TEMPT

TEMPTATION SERIES BOOK ONE

EVELYN BLOOM

EK PUBLISHING INC.

Copyright ©2021 Evelyn Bloom

Published by
EK Publishing Inc.

ISBN#: 978-1-77446-050-4

Edited by
L. Nunn Editing

Cover Art by
EK Designs

TEMPT

TEMPTATION SERIES BOOK ONE

THE BEST PATH FORWARD ISN'T ALWAYS A STRAIGHT LINE.

Ian's life is going sideways.

A messy breakup with his cheating girlfriend and an attraction to co-worker, Will, has him questioning everything – including his sexuality.

Open to discovering the truth, Ian wants to explore his interest in men. More specifically – his interest in Will.

But Ian knows dating a co-worker is a bad idea. When Will makes it clear he isn't looking for a relationship, Ian jumps at the chance to make his biggest fantasy come true.

Too bad his pesky feelings for Will are getting in the way.

Will isn't interested in being someone's test subject. Even if that someone is Ian, the star of Will's secret fantasies.

Been there, done that, has the boot prints on his heart to prove it.

So, why can't he say no to Ian's request?

What's happening between them isn't supposed to mean anything. So, why are Will and Ian connecting in more ways than one? And why does it feel so right?

CHAPTER 1

IAN

"You're breaking up with me?" I dropped into the kitchen chair and stared blankly at my girlfriend. "Are you kidding?"

Lori shook her head. "No, Ian. I'm not."

"But it's almost our anniversary," I said stupidly.

She made that exasperated face that she made so often now and sighed loudly. "What does that have to do with anything?"

"Nothing, I guess," I said.

I stared numbly at her as she shifted her purse on her shoulder. "So, I've already moved my stuff out, but if I've missed anything just text me."

"Just text me? That's it," I said.

She sighed again. "What do you want me to say?"

"Maybe I'm sorry for breaking your heart would be a good place to start."

"Oh please," she snorted. "You're being a drama queen. You're not in love with me – not anymore."

"Why would you say that?" I asked. "I love you, Lori."

"No, you don't," she said simply. "And that's okay. I don't love you anymore either."

"I do love you," I said. "Why do you think I don't?"

"How many times have I asked you to compromise?" she said. "How many times have you just gone ahead and did what you wanted to do? You're a terrible boyfriend, Ian. Selfish and self-centered, and you don't care about me or my needs."

I almost groaned, "this again?" before thinking better of it. This complaint had been a common theme throughout our entire relationship, and while I tried to be open to anything Lori asked, it never seemed to be enough. I hated that I wasn't who Lori wanted me to be.

"I'm trying," I said. "I don't mean to be selfish, but sometimes I don't feel like going out or -"

"You make me stay home all the time," she said. "I'm young, Ian. I have so much life to live, and you keep me holed up in this pathetic condo every weekend."

"That isn't true, and you know it," I said. "Now who's being the drama queen?"

"You're so hurtful," she said.

I took a deep breath. "Me refusing to go to the bar every weekend can't be the reason you're ending it. There has to be something else."

"You're going to make me say it?" she said. "Fine. The sex sucks between us. You don't do it for me anymore, and I don't do it for you. Don't pretend that I do."

"Jesus," I blinked at her, "you're throwing away nearly two years because we're having a dry spell in the sack?"

"It's more than a dry spell, and you know it," she said.

"I'm trying," I said. "I'm open to trying new things."

A weird look crossed Lori's face, and a sick feeling grew in my stomach. "Is this about the other night?"

Lori picked at her fingernails. "No, of course not."

"Look at me, Lori."

She continued to pick at her nails. "It has nothing to do with that."

"Look at me," I repeated.

She lifted her gaze and I said, "I deserve the truth."

She bit her bottom lip as her cheeks reddened. "Okay, yeah, fine, you freaked me out the other night and it was kind of the last straw."

I could feel the colour draining from my own cheeks. "I didn't mean to freak you out. I thought I would try to spice up our sex life."

She laughed bitterly. "Are you hearing yourself? Spice up *our* sex life? No, Ian. That isn't what you were doing. You wanted to try something – something sick and not normal, and I'm not doing that."

Now the colour rushed back into my face. "It's not sick. Plenty of couples do stuff like that and -"

"No, they don't," Lori said. "I asked my girlfriends and not a single one of them has ever had a boyfriend ask them to do that to them."

"You talked to your girlfriends about it?" I said hoarsely as fresh embarrassment rolled through me.

She just shrugged and I glared at her. "That was something private between us."

"Fine, I'm sorry," she said blithely. "But I was freaked out, okay? The first time in months we even try to have sex and you ask me for *that*. I had to talk to someone, and my squad can keep their mouths shut."

"No, they can't," I said. "They're huge gossips."

"At least they're interested in what I have to say," Lori

snapped. "It's not just the sex, Ian. You're not interested in me at all anymore. And asking me to do something in bed that no *normal* guy would ask for is pretty fucking shitty of you, considering you can't even be bothered to ask how my day was half the time."

I wanted to argue with her. I had a leg to stand on in this fight – Lori was rarely home in the evenings anymore and it was pretty hard to have a conversation with someone who was never around. But I was too stunned by the fact that she believed I wasn't normal.

"Lori," I said. "I'm sorry. We can do counseling, and I promise I won't ask you to do anything like that in bed again. I – I didn't realize it would upset you so much, and it was just an idea, you know? I didn't mean anything by it."

"It's too late for counseling. Even if I hadn't been thinking of leaving you, that – that *request* was too much. You're sick, Ian. You need help."

I stared silently at her and she smiled patronizingly. "I'm staying with a friend. Do me a favour and don't try to contact me or see me for the next while, okay? I want this to be a clean break."

My mouth dropped open. "We fucking work together. How am I supposed to not see you?"

She rubbed at her temples in a display of weariness. "Just don't make a scene at work for God's sake."

"Why would I make a scene at work?" I asked.

Her eyes cut to the left and she shifted her purse on her shoulder again. "No reason. Goodbye, Ian. I hope you get the help you need."

"TEN LAPS AROUND THE PERIMETER OF THE GYM. NOW!" I roared.

The twenty-eight tenth grade boys stared at me in a combination of shock and disbelief.

"Are you kidding, Mr. Smith? What for?" One of my more challenging students, Darren Westmore, said.

"Eleven," I said.

"You can't do that!" Darren said.

"Twelve. Care to make it thirteen for you and your class-mates, Mr. Westmore?" I asked.

Darren opened his mouth and the boy next to him punched him hard in the arm. "Darren, shut the fuck up, you idiot," he muttered under his breath.

Darren shut his mouth with a snap as the other boys began to jog around the gym. I heard him mumble, "Who the fuck pissed in his cornflakes this morning?" to one of his buddies and was tempted to add fifty push-ups. Instead, I stalked to my office attached to the gym and slammed the door shut. I leaned against my desk and took several deep breaths. It was only ten-thirty and I was ready to go home and start drinking.

I snorted and rubbed at my aching temple. Not that drinking helped. I'd spent the entire weekend drowning my sorrows, and all that did was leave me with a splitting headache and the worst indigestion of my life. I dropped my hand to my chest and rubbed it instead.

You're sick, Ian. You need help.

Lori's voice echoed in my head. I slammed my fist on my desk. I'd seen Lori at the staff meeting this morning and in the hallway between first and second period. Both times she studiously ignored me, and I did the same. I stared blankly at the floor of my office. It was a small room, there was barely enough space for my desk and my chair, but I was suddenly grateful for the tiny space. At least I could eat my lunch in here and not have to sit in the staff room with Lori.

I scrubbed at the stubble on my jaw. I hadn't shaved this morning and my eyes were still bloodshot from the drinking. I could only imagine what I looked like, and despite showering this morning, even I could smell the beer wafting from my pores. There was a knock on my door, and I turned around as it opened.

"Mr. Smith?"

I forced a smile. "Hello, Mr. Matthews. What can I do for you?"

My stomach did another uneasy flip-flop. I desperately wanted to blame it on the weekend of drinking but couldn't quite get there. Will Matthews taught English, but he looked like a super model. His short dark hair was a direct contrast to my curly blond hair, and where my eyes were a light blue, his were a rich, dark brown. He was two inches taller than my 6'1", and his body was long and lean. I'd seen him at the gym a few times and he was absolutely ripped. I had a pretty respectable six-pack, but Will Matthews sported a freaking eight-pack.

Nearly all of the female teachers drooled over him, and I didn't think there was a single mother in the entire school who missed her appointment with Will Matthews when parent/teacher interviews rolled around. Not that it mattered to him. He didn't go around announcing he was gay, but we all knew. Last year, one of our math teachers, Patty Larken, had seen Will kissing a man at some random Christmas party. It took less than forty-eight hours for her to spread the information. I was surprised the female teachers didn't do a period of mourning when they found out.

"I believe Mr. Jenkins is supposed to be in your class right now."

I stared at the sheepish student standing next to Will. "Why are you late, Alex?"

"I uh, I had to use the bathroom, Mr. Smith," Alex said.

Will turned his icy gaze to Alex and the boy nearly wilted on the spot. "I caught him smoking in the parking lot."

"Weed or cigarettes?" I asked.

"Cigarettes," Will said.

"Alex," I said, "what are you doing, buddy? You know that crap is toxic and if you want to stay on the volleyball team, I need you in top shape. If you're wheezing and falling behind, I'll cut you from the team."

Alex flushed miserably. "I'm sorry, Mr. Smith. I won't do it again."

"Go join the others in running laps," I said.

"Yes, Mr. Smith."

He left my office, and I gave Will a small smile. "Thanks for bringing him to me and not to Joe."

Joe was Joe Anton, our principal. He was a good guy, but he would have suspended, if not outright expelled Alex, for smoking on school property. Considering that Alex was one of my top volleyball players, it would have been a hit for the team.

"You look like hell," Will said, "and you smell like a brewery."

"Excuse me?" I said.

"I know you're upset because you and your girlfriend broke up, but you're not setting a good example for your students."

"How did you know Lori and I broke up?"

"Everyone knows," he said dryly. "Did you think your chatty Cathy ex-girlfriend would keep it quiet?"

"Don't talk about Lori like that," I said automatically.

"Why?" Will challenged.

"Because...just don't," I said.

Will was silent for a moment before saying, "Can I give you a suggestion? Don't try to drink your sorrows away. It never ends well."

"Yeah, thanks," I said.

He looked me up and down, his gaze lingering on my wide chest and flat abdomen. "I've seen you at the gym. You've worked hard to get that body. Don't throw it away with excessive drinking because of a woman who doesn't deserve you."

My mouth dropped open, but Will had already turned and left the office. I felt strange and weirdly too hot. My entire body was tingling, and the way Will had stared at me was disconcerting but not entirely unwelcome.

You're sick, Ian. You need help.

Lori's voice in my head made my heartburn worsen. I yanked open the desk drawer, pulled out a bottle of Tums, and popped two in my mouth.

CHAPTER 2

IAN

One more day. Just one more day – you can do this.

"Ian? Did you hear me?"

I stared blankly at Patty. "No, I'm sorry."

It was Thursday afternoon and the last class of the day had finished half an hour earlier. I was sitting alone in the staff room, telling myself it didn't bother me that I was going home to an empty condo, when Patty Larken walked in.

She smiled and shifted closer on the staff room couch until her thigh pressed against mine. Alarm bells tingled up and down my spine when she rubbed the back of my neck. Her hand was sweaty, and I tried to subtly lean away.

"I said, why don't you come to my place this weekend. I'll make you a home cooked meal. We can't have you starving to death now that you're all by yourself, can we?"

Holy shit. Patty was hitting on me.

Before I could stand up to leave, she grabbed my thigh with her hand. "I know you're lonely, Ian. I am too. I can be discreet, I promise."

"Patty, you have the wrong idea," I said. "I'm not interested in you or anyone right now. It's only been a week since Lori and I broke up and I -"

I made a startled noise when Patty practically threw her body over mine and kissed me. Shocked by her boldness, I sat passively still as she sucked on my bottom lip then stuck her tongue in my mouth. The sound of someone clearing their throat behind us knocked me out of my stunned state.

I pushed Patty away. She made a soft squeak of surprise and rubbed at her arms. "That hurt, Ian. God, you don't have to be so rough."

I flushed. I was a big guy and I immediately felt horrible that I had hurt her. "Patty, I -"

"Maybe you should have respected his personal boundaries."

I whipped my head around and groaned inwardly. Will Matthews stood behind us. I jumped up off the couch as Patty snorted.

"Bugger off, Will."

"This is your place of business, Patty. Try to be professional, would you?"

Patty rose gracefully to her feet and smoothed her skirt. "Never thought a man whore like you would be such a prude. From what I hear, you'll fuck anything that moves."

"You know that isn't true," Will said. "I didn't fuck you when you begged me to, did I?"

Patty flushed bright red and gave Will a venomous look. "You're an asshole."

Will just smiled at her as Patty turned to me with a strained smile. "If you change your mind, Ian, you know where to find me."

I didn't reply. With another angry look at Will, Patty flounced out of the staff room.

"Thanks," I said.

Will just shrugged and glanced at his watch. "Why are you still here?"

"No reason. Just didn't feel like going home." I waited for his sympathetic reply. Over the last few days, Lori had made it perfectly clear to the other teachers that she had broken up with me. Consequently, I'd been receiving a lot of sympathetic looks.

Is it sympathy? It feels more like pity. They're all acting weird around you now, Ian. You know they are.

I shoved my inner voice out of my head. Maybe they knew what I had asked Lori to do in the bedroom, or maybe they didn't. Either way, I had enough issues right now, and I didn't need to add paranoia to the list.

Will hadn't said a word. I raised my gaze to his. There was no sympathy in his dark eyes, but there wasn't pity either. In fact, it almost looked like he was...

Nope. No way. Uh-uh. Just because Will was gay didn't mean that he lusted after me. Thinking shit like that – that a gay man lusted after every man they met – was what goddamn homophobes did. And I wasn't a homophobe.

No, but maybe you want Will to lust after you. Maybe you want to know what it's like to –

Christ on a pony, if my fucking inner voice didn't shut the fuck up soon, I was going to rip it right out of my head and throttle it. I wasn't bisexual. I wasn't gay. I was straight. I loved women. End of story.

Is it though? What you asked Lori to do – that isn't something that a straight guy asks for. The look on her face when you said it ... fuck, man, you should have known then that she was going to leave you.

"Ian?"

Sweat was beading up on my forehead and I couldn't

seem to stop the shaking in my hands. I closed my eyes, took four deep breaths, and forced a smile on my face.

"Sorry. It's been a long week."

"Yes, I imagine it has been."

I opened my eyes and nodded curtly. "Good night, Mr. Matthews. I'll see you tomorrow."

"Good night, Mr. Smith," he said.

I hurried out of the staff room and walked down the empty hallway toward the front entrance. I released my breath in a shaky exhale. Fuck, what was wrong with me?

Ooh, I know the answer! My inner voice crowed cheerfully. *Let's see – it probably started three weeks ago when you had that sex dream about none other than Will Matthews. Then when you finally accepted that your dream of having Will's cock shoved in your ass made you hotter than fucking fire, you had a little too much to drink one night and asked your girlfriend to fuck your ass with a strap-on. One week later, your girlfriend of two years – the woman you thought you would marry – dumped you for being a sick pervert.*

I groaned inwardly as my inner voice said, *Cheer up, big guy. It could have been worse – you could have told Lori you wanted her to pretend she was Will while she fucked you in the ass.*

My blood ran cold at the thought. What would Lori have done or said if she even suspected that I was suddenly lusting after the grade twelve English teacher? It was bad enough that –

"Stop it, you bad boy."

I froze mid-step. Lost in thought, I had missed the door to the stairwell and carried right on toward the art department. As a high-pitched and very familiar giggle drifted to me, my guts clenched, and my heart hammered in my chest.

Numb and oddly disconnected, I shoved open the door to

the art room. Lori was standing by her desk, and she giggled again as the man lifted her up and plunked her down on the desk. He stepped between her open thighs and I watched in disbelief as he stuck his hand up her skirt and grabbed her crotch. Lori moaned and her back arched. They kissed deeply, and Lori clutched at his ass as he rubbed furiously between her legs.

"Oh baby," she moaned when he released her mouth. "Oh God, you'd better stop before I cum all over my desk. You'd better – what the hell?"

She jerked wildly as she caught sight of me standing in the doorway. She pushed at the man's arm, and he stared irritably at her. "What?"

"It's Ian!" Lori snapped.

The man pulled his hand out from under her skirt and turned around. He cleared his throat before smiling nervously at me. "Uh, hey, Ian."

"Hello, Frank," I said.

"Uh, how are you?"

"Considering I just caught the chemistry teacher finger fucking my ex-girlfriend in her classroom, I'd say I've had better days."

"Ian, don't freak out," Lori said as she slid off the desk. She straightened her skirt and tossed back her hair.

I cocked my head and took a few steps into the room. Frank made a nervous stay-back gesture before moving behind Lori.

"Don't freak out?" I said. "That's what you said to me the day you broke up with me. Wasn't it? You asked me not to freak out. I asked you why I would, but you didn't say."

"It's over between us," Lori said.

"Yeah, I know," I retorted as I walked steadily toward them. "But I guess what I'm trying to figure out now is whether you and old Frank here were fucking while we were still a couple."

"Of course, we weren't. Don't be ridiculous," Lori said. Her eyes cut to the left.

"You always were a terrible liar, Lori."

"It's none of your business!" I was standing in front of her now and she poked me hard in the chest.

"None of my business? You were fucking someone else behind my back and it's none of my business?"

There was a weird buzzing in my ears and that odd feeling of disconnect was back and stronger than ever. I stared over Lori's shoulder at Frank. His eyes were wide and frightened looking, and he made a low sound of fear when I grinned at him.

"Move, Lori," I said. "I need to have a man-to-man with Frank."

"No," she said. "You don't need to talk to him at all. Just get out of here and – hey! Put me down!"

She smacked me in the chest as I put my hands around her waist and very gently lifted her and set her down to the side. Frank put up his hands and said defensively, "Listen, she came on to me, okay? I didn't set out to fuck her when she was still your woman, but she was relentless. She – she wouldn't take no for an answer and -"

"You asshole!" Lori bleated behind me. "You fucking came on to me!"

"Shut up, you stupid bitch," Frank said.

"Call her a bitch again and I'll knock your teeth out," I said.

He flushed bright red and stared scornfully at me. "You think she's going to take you back if you defend her honour? She's been spreading nothin' but shit about you for months, buddy. Besides, she wouldn't have needed to come to me for sex if you could have satisfied her in bed like a real man. Maybe if you had concentrated on her needs instead of wondering what it would be like to take it up the ass, she wouldn't have -"

My barely contained self-control shattered. Frank made a frightened *eep* when I grabbed him by the shoulders and shoved him into the whiteboard. He swung wildly at me. I dodged it easily and punched him in the stomach as Lori screamed shrilly.

"Stop it, Ian! Stop it right now! You'll kill him!"

I yanked the wheezing, gasping Frank into a standing position and balled my hand into a fist. I wasn't even close to killing him, but our chemistry teacher was about to lose his fucking front teeth.

See how well he does at picking up the women without his teeth, I thought petulantly.

Before I could punch him in the face, a hard arm slipped around my neck and pulled up tight. I gagged and clawed at the arm as my unknown attacker dragged me away from Frank and toward the front door.

"Enough, Ian!"

Will's low voice in my ear made me freeze, but he didn't release his grip around my throat. Instead, he moved me easily to the door as Lori whirled around to face us.

"You fucking asshole, Ian!" She was crying loudly as she slipped her arm around the still-wheezing Frank. "You could have killed him!"

"Fuck you!" I shouted. The red haze of anger still surrounded me in a thick cloud. Will's arm tightened mercilessly around my neck when I struggled against him. "You're goddamn lucky I didn't kill him! You're lucky that I -"

"I said enough!" Will snarled into my ear.

He dragged me out of the room and down the hallway. I

fought bitterly against him and he muttered a curse before opening a door and shoving me inside. It was pitch black and I stumbled into the wall, banging my shin on something hard and unyielding as Will stepped in after me and slammed the door shut.

"Get the fuck off of me!" I shouted when Will grabbed my wrists. He yanked them over my head and pinned my arms against the wall as he pressed his large body against mine. I tried to headbutt him and he dodged it easily before slamming me against the wall.

"Calm down," he said quietly into my ear. I renewed my struggle, surging my big body up against his. Despite my power, I couldn't break free of his grip. I grunted and thrashed and swore a blue streak as Will held me against the wall. Finally, after almost five minutes, I collapsed against the wall. I was breathing heavily, my chest heaving for each breath of oxygen.

"Better?" Will said into my ear.

A little shiver went down my back. "Yeah, you can let go."

He released me cautiously but didn't step back, instead letting his upper body rest lightly against mine as I rubbed at my wrists. There was only a thin crack of light beneath the door, but my vision had adjusted, and I could make out some of his features despite the darkness.

"Are we in the janitor's closet?" I could smell cleaning supplies and there was a vague mop-like shape to my left.

"Yes."

"Great," I muttered. "Excuse me."

"Hold on." One hard hand pushed me square in the chest until I was pinned against the wall again. I should have knocked his hand away, but Will's touch was making me tremble. I could almost feel the heat of his hand burning into my chest.

"Let me go," I said unconvincingly.

"You need to calm down first."

"I'm calm," I snapped. My emotions were out of fucking control. The faint thread of lust I was feeling for Will was being overshadowed by the return of my anger. Lori was fucking Frank – the goddamn chemistry teacher.

"You're not," Will said.

"Fuck you!" I said. "I think finding out my ex-girlfriend was fucking around on me while we were dating is more than enough reason to be angry."

"Do you think beating up a co-worker and getting fired will help your situation?" Will asked.

My temper flared. I hated that he was so rational and calm. Of course, he was – he wasn't the one being called sick. He wasn't the one whose girlfriend found him so repulsive that she fucked another guy.

I shoved Will hard in the chest. He grunted in surprise and stumbled back. I tried to push my way past him and yelped when Will slammed me up against the wall. His hand closed lightly around my throat and he pressed his hard body against mine before lowering his mouth to my ear.

"Don't do that again, Ian."

I tried to surge forward. We grappled briefly before I found myself with my arms pinned above my head again, Will's hands holding my wrists captive as I bucked my body against his.

"All those rippling muscles," Will said with a low laugh, "and I can still overpower you. Does that bother you?"

"No," I admitted as I ceased struggling again. "I know how strong you are."

"Do you?" he said.

"Yes, I've watched you at the gym."

"I know," he said.

His warm breath washed over my mouth and I couldn't stop the full body shiver or – God help me – the way my cock hardened.

"You watch me a lot, Ian. Did you think I wouldn't notice?" he said.

"I don't – I mean, I watch you a regular amount," I said.

He laughed, and my cock went from half-mast to fully erect. Fuck, what was happening to me?

"A regular amount," he said. Leaving one hand around my wrists, he used the other to trace across my chest.

I could have pulled free, he wasn't powerful enough to hold me against the wall with one hand, but I couldn't – didn't want to – move. Will's hand slipped across my chest, his pinky finger brushing against my pebbled nipple through the thin material of my t-shirt.

The moan slipped out before I could stop it. Will cocked his head and studied my mouth as his hand trailed down my abdomen. His fingers curled into the waistband of my track-pants, and I moaned again when he tugged my pelvis forward and I felt the hard length of his cock.

Despite knowing he could feel my own erection, I said, "I watch you for... work out tips."

Fuck me. I sounded like an idiot.

Will laughed again. I gasped when one finger slipped beneath my waistband to touch the trail of hair below my belly button.

"Work out tips, huh?" he said. "So, you're telling me you don't watch me because you're wondering what it would be like to have my tongue in your mouth?"

I swallowed hard, my gaze dropping to his perfect mouth.

He teased my treasure trail and precum dripped from my cock to wet my briefs.

"Wondering what it would be like to have my hand wrapped around your cock?" Will said. "My dick in your ass?"

I groaned and, madness coursing through my veins, pressed my mouth against Will's. He pushed me back against the wall and took control of the kiss, angling his mouth over mine. I parted my lips, moaning at the first taste of his tongue in my mouth. He explored and tasted, his firm lips and wet tongue shoving any thoughts of my cheating ex right out of my head.

I returned his kiss eagerly. He tasted like mint and sin and everything I'd ever wanted. I cried out into his mouth when his hand slipped inside my underwear and wrapped around my cock. He jacked me with hard, perfect strokes as his tongue teased my mouth.

Will still had my arms pinned over my head, and he made a low groan of approval when I arched into his hand. He released my mouth and studied my straining body.

"Fuck, you're so damn hot," he muttered as he jacked me faster. "Cum for me, Ian. Show me what you look like when you're cumming in my hand."

I groaned, my hips pumping against his hand. I was so close already. My lack of control was both terrifying and exhilarating. When was the last time I'd cum simply from a hand job? I couldn't remember, but my balls were tightening, and my cock was swelling, and there was no denying that I was on the very edge.

When Will released my wrists and pinched my flat nipple through my shirt, I sailed over that edge and into perfect bliss. I fucking exploded into his hand, my cum spurting out to coat his hand and the front of my briefs. Will's hand clamped across my mouth, muffling my shout of pleasure as rope after rope of hot cum flew from my cock.

My body shaking, I collapsed against the wall, sucking in a lungful of air when Will released my mouth. I watched with growing embarrassment as Will pulled a handkerchief from one pocket and used it to wipe his hand clean before handing it to me.

My shame suddenly coated me in a thick layer. I turned my back and used Will's handkerchief to wipe away the sticky cum coating my cock and briefs. It helped a little but not enough that I wouldn't have to haul ass to my car before a wet spot leaked through to the front of my pants.

Cheeks burning and my face bright red, I turned to face Will, clenching the now wet fabric in my hand. For a second I almost tried to hand it to him before common sense kicked in. I shoved it into the front pocket of my track pants.

My gaze dropped to the front of Will's pants. His erection was obvious, and more heat invaded my cheeks. Fuck. I needed to return the favour, but now that I'd cum, my over-heated brain was starting to function again, and confusion and shame were vying for space in my head.

I'd just let another man give me a hand job at my goddamn place of work. I'd kissed him and let him stick his hand down my pants and…

I stared at Will and whatever he saw on my face turned the satisfaction in his eyes to regret. I swallowed hard as he took a step back.

"Fuck," he said. "This was a mistake."

"Will, I …"

Why did it bother me to hear him say it was a mistake?

"No," he said curtly. "I shouldn't have done that. If you want to report me to Joe, I'll understand completely."

I stared at him before shaking my head. "I'm not going to

report you to Joe. Jesus, Will. You think I want people knowing what just happened?"

His face twisted before a mask fell over it. I groaned inwardly and said, "No, wait, that isn't what I meant. I didn't _"

"It's fine," he said. He backed away, reaching for the door and opening it slightly. He glanced left and then right before giving me a quick look. "We both forget this ever happened. Good night, Mr. Smith."

"Will, wait, I…"

He was gone before I could explain what I'd meant.

CHAPTER 3

WILL

I scrubbed my hand across my jaw. I hadn't shaved this morning which wasn't like me, but after too many sleepless nights, I'd said fuck it. It was Friday. If Joe or any of the other administrators wanted to speak to me about some stubble, they'd find out real quick what I fucking thought of them.

I muttered a curse and cleaned off the whiteboard with short angry strokes. My students had borne the brunt of my bad mood all week, and as an apology, I'd given them a rare homework free weekend. That had cheered them up considerably. When the bell rang, most of them even managed to say goodbye to me as they were escaping my classroom.

I continued to swipe at the whiteboard even though it was as clean as it was gonna get. I'd barely been able to do my job the last few days. I was too consumed by thoughts of Ian Smith and his goddamn mouth to concentrate.

Not just his mouth, buddy. Let's not forget about that thick dick of his, or the way he moaned when your hand was

wrapped around said thick dick. And that fucking ass of his.
You want to be balls deep inside of it. Admit it.

My dick was hardening, and I adjusted myself with a grimace. Thinking about Ian was a very bad fucking idea, but one I couldn't seem to stop doing. I'd had my suspicions about Ian for a while, call it that stupid fucking gaydar or whatever you wanted, but when he'd joined my gym a few months back, my suspicions were confirmed.

No one who was perfectly straight looked at a man like Ian looked at me.

Doesn't mean he's gay.

No, it didn't. Which was why I'd ignored those looks and my own attraction to him. The last thing I needed was to fuck some confused, in a relationship with a woman, co-worker who didn't know if he was straight, gay, or bisexual.

And no matter how attracted I was to Ian, the man definitely didn't know what the fuck he wanted. Other than making sure people didn't know he was attracted to me.

My stomach churned at the memory of Ian's face after he'd cum in my hand. The shame, the fear that others would find out... I knew that look too intimately, had tried to live with it for too long, and I was never doing it again.

I didn't broadcast my sexual preferences to my coworkers or the rest of the world, but I didn't hide it either and never would again. Three years of loving a man who refused to leave the closet and kept me holed up in there with him, had convinced me never to date anyone who wasn't out. It didn't matter how fucking hot the guy was, or if I'd had too many fantasies to count of him on his knees in front of me, his mouth full of my cock.

I'd made one fuck of a mistake with Ian last week, but even now I couldn't bring myself to completely regret dragging him out of that room. And not just because I didn't want him being fired over his asshole of an ex-girlfriend cheating on him. Kissing Ian, watching his face as he came in my hand would be my favourite jerk off fantasy for years.

Even if it had happened in a literal closet.

More of a janitor's nook, really.

"Christ," I muttered to myself as I stared at the clean whiteboard. "You took advantage of his emotional melt-down and his attraction to you just so you could get a taste of him. You know what that makes you, right? The biggest asshole on the planet."

"Who's the biggest asshole on the planet?"

I froze before turning to stare at the doorway, the tendons in my neck creaking like old floorboards. Ian was standing in the entrance to my classroom and I drank him in greedily. He was wearing his usual outfit of a t-shirt and track pants and the t-shirt was sticking to his flat abdomen.

He caught me staring and pulled his shirt from his stomach self-consciously. I almost groaned out loud when I caught a glimpse of that perfect treasure trail before his shirt fell back into place.

"I just finished a run with my last class of the day." He sniffed at his armpit. "I probably stink. Sorry."

I set the whiteboard eraser on the ledge. My desire to pin Ian against the wall and bury my face in his pit was almost overwhelming. I clenched my jaw and shoved my hands into my pockets. Christ, it was like I *wanted* to be arrested for sexual harassment in the workplace.

"Is this a bad time?" Ian looked nervous and unsure.

I glanced at my watch. "I was just headed to the gym."

"Right," he said. "This will only take a minute."

He glanced behind him and when he started to shut the door to my classroom, I said sharply, "Leave it open."

He jerked at my harsh tone but left it open before

approaching me cautiously. "So, uh, who's the biggest asshole on the planet?"

"Me," I said. "What can I do for you, Mr. Smith?"

A muscle ticked rapidly in his jaw as he shoved his hand into his front pocket and pulled out my handkerchief. "I wanted to return this. I, uh, washed it."

His face flushed red. I ignored how fucking adorable it was as I snatched the handkerchief from him, being careful not to touch his fingers. "Thanks."

He stared quietly at me and I made my voice impatient. "Is that everything, Mr. Smith?"

"No." His Adam's apple bobbed as he swallowed a couple of times like he was working up the courage to speak. "I wanted to clarify what I said in the janitor's closet last week."

"No need to explain," I said briskly. "It was perfectly clear what you meant."

"No, it wasn't," he said. "Can you just listen for one fucking minute instead of acting like you can't stand the sight of me?"

I rubbed the back of my neck. "Sorry. I'm not – I don't... what is it you wanted to say?"

"When I said I didn't want people to know what happened, it's not because of... of the gay thing, but because of the inappropriateness of letting someone jack me off in a closet at my place of employment. Whether that person is male or female," he finished hastily. "It has nothing to do with you or, uh, whatever confusion I might be feeling right now."

"Doesn't it?" I said.

"No." He chewed fiercely at his bottom lip until I wanted to go to him and stop his lip torture with a kiss. "I mean, maybe a little, but it's definitely not the biggest reason."

We stared silently at each other for almost a minute. The sound of the wall clock ticking was the only noise in the room. I looked away from his pretty blue eyes, my throat dry and every muscle in my body tense. "Thank you for explaining. Have a good weekend, Mr. Smith."

"Do you want to go for a drink later tonight?" Ian said.

My gaze whipped back to his in a hurry. The shock on my face brought a fresh flush to his cheeks. "Just a drink. I know this great little pub over on -"

"No," I said.

Hurt flashed across his face. I admired his bravery when he said, "I'd like to get to know you better."

"That's nice, but I'm not interested in dating someone who doesn't know if they're straight or gay," I said. "Nor do I want to be someone's rebound."

I waited for him to get pissed but he just nodded and said, "That's fair. Have a good weekend, Will."

"You as well, Mr. Smith."

I waited until he left before I collapsed into my desk chair and stared blankly at my laptop. Every part of me screamed to chase him down the damn hallway and agree to the drink.

But that was madness.

———

"HUH. SO, YOU WERE RIGHT. HE IS GAY." TRISTAN TOOK A swig of beer.

"Not necessarily," I said. "Besides, did you hear the part where I took advantage of him?"

"You said he kissed you first," Tristan pointed out.

"Yeah, but…"

"But what?"

I just shook my head and took a swallow of beer. I'd

taken advantage of Ian's emotional state and we all knew it. Rehashing it repeatedly just made me nauseous.

"I don't think it's that big of a deal," Tristan said. "Ian didn't seem traumatized this afternoon, right? I mean, the guy asked you out on a date."

I rubbed at my forehead. "He didn't ask me out on a date, he asked me to go for a beer."

Tristan rolled his eyes. "Jesus, that's a date, you asshole. Has it been so long since you've been on one that you forget how they work?"

"Fuck off," I said.

My best friend laughed and clapped me on the back. "There's a hint of the Will I know and love."

"What's that supposed to mean?" I said.

He drank some beer before saying, "Just that you haven't been the same since Mike."

"Since we broke up, you mean," I said.

"Nope. I said what I meant."

I studied him in the dim light of the pub, ignoring the din of conversation around us. "Actually, you're being really fucking obtuse, and I hate it."

Tristan studied me across the table, his dark eyes unreadable. "It means that dating Mike and having to hide it, changed you. And I didn't particularly care for that version of Will. It makes me happy to see old Will starting to shine through again."

I slumped in my seat, picking at the label on my beer bottle. "Why didn't you say something to me before this?"

"Because you loved Mike and believed he made you happy. I wanted you to be happy, buddy, I really did." He ran a hand through his short dark hair. "Besides, if I'd tried to tell you that Mike was bad for you, you would have told me to fuck right off and never talked to me again."

I frowned at him. "I wouldn't have. We've been best friends since high school, Tristan. I wouldn't toss you over some guy."

"You loved Mike," he said.

"I also love you," I said.

"Aw," he fluttered his remarkably long eyelashes at me, "I love you too, Billy."

"You're such a fucking twat," I said.

He laughed and held his beer bottle up. I clinked mine against his and we both took a long drink. He glanced around the pub before saying, "What are you going to do about this Ian thing?"

"Nothing," I said. "There is no Ian thing. He's a co-worker and -"

"Obviously, there's no rule against dating a co-worker if he was dating this Lori chick," Tristan said.

"He's a co-worker," I repeated loudly, "and he doesn't know what he wants or who he is."

"You could help him figure it out," Tristan said.

"I'm not getting stuck in the closet with some guy ever again," I said moodily.

"Doesn't sound like Ian's that type of guy. I mean, he specifically said it wasn't the gay thing he didn't want people to know about."

"He doesn't even know if he's gay or straight... and I'm not interested in helping him figure it out."

"Because you want more from him and you're afraid he'll just use you for a little experimentation," Tristan said.

I hesitated, but if I couldn't be honest with Tristan then who could I be honest with? "Yeah."

"Then it's better to not have anything to do with him," Tristan said.

"I know."

"Sorry, buddy." Tristan's look of sympathy only made me feel marginally better.

"Thanks. Anyway, enough of my shit. How's the new job going?"

"Good." Tristan studied his hands. There was the tiniest bit of grease still embedded in his knuckles. "Worked on a classic Aston Martin today."

"Sweet. Shepherd still being an asshole?"

"Yep."

"You still want to fuck him?"

"Yep."

"Shitty," I said.

Tristan shrugged. "Having a crush on your boss is annoying. Having a crush on your boss who hates your guts is ridiculous."

"Can't help who your cock is attracted to," I said.

"Ain't that the fucking truth," Tristan said.

"Besides, I doubt he hates you. He wouldn't have hired you if he did," I said.

"He hired me because he was desperate and because Jimmy gave me such a glowing review," Tristan said.

"Which you deserve," I replied.

"I know. I'm good at my job, but, apparently, I pissed in Shepherd's cornflakes that first day and I have no fucking idea how."

"You worried he's gonna fire you?"

Tristan mused that over before shaking his head. "Nah. He gives me all of the classic cars to work on and Roger says that's unheard of. Normally Shepherd doesn't trust anyone but himself to work on them. The client who brings them in is some kind of millionaire, and is particular about who works on his cars. So, Shepherd knows I'm a good mechanic and trusts me, but hates who I am as a person."

"Maybe it's an 'I want to fuck you, so I pretend to hate you', type of deal," I said.

"Nah, I'm not his type. Richie says he likes twinks."

I studied the chipped black polish on his nails. "You're twink-ish."

He laughed. "Like hell I am. Anyway, I know it's early, but I gotta go."

He pulled his wallet out of his pocket and I shook my head. "I've got this."

"You've always 'got this'." Tristan's voice was low and defeated sounding.

"Hey," I leaned forward, "it's all good, buddy. You know I don't mind."

"I mind," he said. "I hate being a charity case."

"You're not a charity case, and besides, it's not your fault. It's your father's fault. It's a real dick move for him to demand you pay him back just because you refused to bend to his will."

Tristan nodded, although he didn't look convinced. "Thanks, man. Listen, don't sit here and drink by yourself."

"I won't," I said. "I'll finish this one and go home."

I knew Tristan didn't believe me, but he didn't push the matter. "I'll text you later tomorrow."

"Yeah, okay," I said.

He slid out of the booth and fist bumped me before leaving. I stared at my beer, my thoughts turning back to Ian and his perfect mouth almost instantaneously. Irritated with myself, I sucked back a huge mouthful of beer, swallowing it down as the server stopped at the booth.

"Another one?" He picked up Tristan's empty bottle and set it on his tray.

I hesitated. I'd told Tristan I would go home, but the

thought of sitting in my empty house was more fucking depressing than drinking alone.

"Sure," I said.

CHAPTER 4

IAN

"You sure you're okay?" Rachel nudged me with her elbow.

"I'm fine." I shifted on the barstool, nodding to the bartender when he set the beer in front of me.

"Fine like wine," Rachel said before laughing at her own terrible joke.

"Rach, honey, don't take this the wrong way, but your jokes are not funny," I said.

"Ouch," she said. "Who pooped in your granola this morning?"

"Gross." I stared morosely at the bar, tracing my finger around and around the drink ring ghosted into the wood. Blackmoore's Pub was one of my favourite places, but I couldn't shake the melancholy that had dropped over me ever since Will had so quickly and concisely shut down my fumbling attempt to ask him out.

"It was probably for the best," Rachel said.

"What?"

"Will not going out with you," she said like she'd read my fucking mind.

She probably had. We'd been best friends since we were kids, and no one knew me as well as Rachel.

She held up her hand and ticked off each point on perfectly manicured fingers. "One, you're co-workers, and you've discovered the hard way that dating a co-worker is kind of terrible. Two, you're not even sure if you're gay or bisexual or just gay for Will. Three, you're still getting over a long-term relationship."

"I know," I said.

She rested her head on my shoulder for a moment. "I'm sorry you're sad, honey. I hate that you're confused and hurting. Also, I really want to punch that cunt Lori right in her babymaker for what she did to you."

"She didn't do anything to me," I said.

She scowled at me. "Bullshit. She made you feel bad for a perfectly *normal* request, then used it as an excuse to break up with you, when the real reason was that she couldn't keep a fucking chemistry teacher's dick out of her cooch. A fucking chemistry teacher! She might as well just fuck a beaker."

I burst into laughter despite my depression. Rachel grinned at me before taking a sip of her rum and coke.

I drank some beer and gave her a side look. "What I requested wasn't normal, Rachel. Not for a straight guy."

"You'd be surprised." She shrugged. "It's normal for someone who's gay."

"I don't know if I'm gay."

"You don't know if you're not," she said. "Or you could be bi. Who the fuck cares either way?"

"I care," I said. "I care because…"

"Because why?"

"Because not knowing who or what I want is confusing as hell."

"You know you want Will Matthews," Rachel said.

"He doesn't want me."

"Eh… doesn't he, though?" she said.

I groaned. "I don't even fucking know anymore. What if I am gay or bi?"

"What if you are?" Rachel said.

"What will people say?"

"Are you really worried about that?"

I hesitated before shaking my head. "No. At least not with the people who matter, like you and my folks. The three of you will love me no matter what."

"Fuckin' A we will, my friend," Rachel said. She toasted me with her glass before taking a sip. "First things first, we need to find out if you're actually gay or just gay for Will."

"I hate that saying," I said. "Can someone really just be gay for one person?"

"I think so," she said. "I'm as straight as a toothpick, but I'd still let Angela Bassett have her naughty, naughty way with me if she was so inclined."

I laughed and Rachel took another sip of her drink. "Okay, this will require one hundred percent honesty, Ian, even if you find it embarrassing. What's on your porn browser history?"

"What do you mean?" I tried to sound confused even as my face reddened.

"One hundred percent honesty," Rachel reminded me. "How much gay porn is on your browser history?"

"A lot," I said.

"Okay. In the past, have you ever been attracted to a guy other than Will Matthews?"

I studied my amber bottle of beer, working my way past

Lori's voice in my head that kept repeating I was sick. "Yeah," I admitted. In university, I had a crush on a guy in one of my classes."

"What type of crush?" Rachel pressed. "A, hey that guy's good looking and sometimes I get a tingling in my crotch area when he's near me, crush? Or a, I'm masturbating to thoughts of him naked six times a week, crush."

I swallowed hard. "The second one."

"And you never told me about this," Rachel said disapprovingly. "What the hell, Ian?"

"It felt weird to admit it," I said. "I didn't think you would judge me or anything, but I didn't know how to express it or even if it meant anything. Until Will, he's the only guy I've crushed on."

"Ever done ass play on yourself?" Rachel said.

My face flamed bright red. "No."

"Okay. Not that it means anything because, dude, there are plenty of straight guys who like ass play and pegging," Rachel said.

"According to Lori, I'm sick and I need help," I said.

"Yeah, well, that cunt is a raging homophobe, and she and her bigoted views can tongue kiss my bleached asshole," Rachel said.

I laughed. "I love you. Also, stop bleaching your butthole."

"I like the way it looks."

"Why are you staring at your own anus?" I said.

She just laughed before sobering. "You remember Evan?"

"The football player you dated last year for about three months?"

"That's the one. He was straight and also super into ass play. I pegged him at least half a dozen times. So, Lori calling you sick for asking for some pegging, is just her exposing her homophobia."

Hearing Rachel talk about pegging a guy like it was no big deal, loosened the knot in my stomach. Apparently, asking to be pegged was more normal than I thought.

"You're not a freak, Ian. You know that, right?"

"Yeah, deep down, I do," I said. "I just... this is super confusing for me right now."

"I know it is. I think we need to find you a guy who's willing to let you," she paused, "I don't want to say experiment because that sounds sketchy, but you know what I mean. Find someone you're attracted to who isn't looking for anything serious and have him show you the ropes of gay sex."

"There are ropes in gay sex?"

"Honey, there are ropes in all sorts of sex," Rachel said with a grin. "Seriously though, you want to know what it's like to be with a guy, right?"

I paused. Did I? Or did I just want to know what it was like to be with Will Matthews? I mused it over for a bit. Rachel sat quietly beside me, sipping her drink and letting me think, while she ignored the horny looks from the men also sitting at the bar.

"Yes," I finally said. "I want to know what it's like."

A weight lifted off my chest. The act of acknowledging my desire, of no longer pretending that it was just a weird crush on one guy, was decidedly freeing. Not that I wasn't still horny as hell for Will, but that ship had definitely sailed, so why not try to find someone else?

Because it's Will you want.

Maybe, but he didn't want someone who was confused and unsure, and I would respect that.

"Okay," Rachel said. "So, we take you to Sapphire's and find you a guy."

"Do you think a gay bar is the way to go?" I said.

"Well, it's either that or a dating app," Rachel said. "Your choice."

"I'll have to think about it," I said. "I'm not sure which is the better idea and honestly -"

"Watch the fuck where you're going, dickhead!"

Rachel and I swiveled on our seats at the angry shout. My jaw dropped. Without stopping to think about it, I slid off my stool and stepped between Will and the tattooed man staring angrily at him.

"Ian?" Will stared blearily at me before grinning. "Hey, man. How the fuck are you?"

"Good," I said. I pressed my hand against his chest and smiled apologetically at the fuming man standing in front of us. "Sorry about that."

"He fucking spilled my drink. Asshole," the man snarled.

"Fuck you," Will said with a lazy grin. "You bumped into me."

"You fucker!" The man started forward, and I shoved him back with one hard hand.

"Step back, buddy."

The man glared at me, but I didn't budge. He was shorter than me, and while he was well-muscled, I could hold my own in a fight if I had to.

"He's drunk," I said to the man. "It was an accident."

"He spilled my fucking drink," the man repeated.

"We'll buy you a fresh one." Rachel had appeared and she smiled at the guy. "C'mon, big guy, you really want to end the night in a fight? Besides, my friend here occasionally fights dirty."

The man grunted and rolled his eyes. Rachel's grin

widened. "Follow me to the bar and I'll buy your drink right now."

"Yeah, okay," he said.

I breathed a sigh of relief, keeping my hand on Will's chest as Rachel led the guy to the bar. She bought him a drink, shook his hand, and made her way back to Will and me.

"So, this is Will, huh?" Rachel looked him up and down. "He's as cute as you said he was."

"Thanks!" Will grinned at her – he was kind of adorable when he was drunk – and held out his hand. "Who are you?"

"I'm Ian's best friend, Rachel." She shook his hand, laughing when Will brought her hand to his mouth and kissed her knuckles.

"Nice to meetcha'." Will swayed on his feet. I hooked my arm around his waist, trying to ignore the feel of his perfect muscled body against mine.

"How much have you had to drink?" I asked.

He shrugged. "Dunno. A few. After Tristan left, I lost track a little."

"Tristan?" Weirdly intense jealousy was already unfurling in my stomach.

"*My* best friend," Will said before sagging against me. "Fuck, I'm dizzy. I gotta find a cab or call an Uber."

"You need to drive him home, Ian," Rachel said. "You've only had half a beer and with the state he's in, he'll probably pass out in the Uber or on his front lawn."

"Will?" I squeezed his waist and he smiled at me before running his fingers over my chest. "I'm gonna drive you home, okay?"

"Sure. It'll give me a chance to have another go at your gorgeous dick," he said with a flirty grin.

My face turned bright red as Rachel laughed. "Nothing more beautiful than a horny English teacher."

"Thanks," Will said. "Let's go, Ian. I'll suck your dick if you suck mine."

"Oh, he's so naughty. I love it!" Rachel said as I helped Will toward the exit.

We walked slowly down the street toward the lot I'd parked in, Will mostly leaning against me. I helped him into the front seat, gritting my teeth and ignoring my stiffening cock when Will kissed my neck as I was buckling him in.

I straightened and closed the car door. "Get in, Rachel, I'll give you a ride home too."

"Nope," she said as she texted on her phone. "Tabitha and Mark are on their way here. I'm meeting up with them."

"You sure?"

"Positive." She stood on her tiptoes and planted a kiss on my lips. "Have fun getting your dick sucked, honey."

I glared at her. "That's not going to happen. Will's drunk and I'm not taking advantage of him."

She smiled at me and kissed me again. "You're the best guy I know, Ian. Love you."

"Love you too. You okay to walk back to the pub?"

She nodded. "Dude, it's less than a block away. I'm good. Besides, I'm the one with the black belt, remember?"

"True," I said. "You are tougher than me."

"Fucking right I am," she said. "Bye, babe. Text me tomorrow."

"I will. Bye, Rach."

CHAPTER 5

IAN

Weirdly, Will's house wasn't that far from my condo. A small navy coloured bungalow with a wide front porch and lush flowerbeds planted in front of it, the place looked warm and inviting. I helped him up the porch steps and opened the screen door.

"Keys?" I asked.

"In my pocket." Will grinned at me but made no effort to get them.

"Will," I said.

"Ian," he said.

"Give me your keys."

"You want 'em, you get 'em," he said with a cute grin.

I sighed. "Right or left?"

He wiggled his hips at me. "You're gonna have to go fishing for yourself, handsome."

I had to look away so he wouldn't see my grin. I cleared my throat and, my hand trembling slightly, reached into Will's front right pocket. My fingers brushed against his keys

– thank fucking God – but goosebumps broke out on my flesh when I also brushed against Will's erect cock and he moaned.

Swallowing hard and breathing fast, I yanked his keys free. "Which one?"

"That one." Will pointed to the only silver one. I shoved the key into the lock, making a high-pitched squeak when Will's hand squeezed my ass.

"Fuck, your ass is incredible," he mumbled as I opened the door. We staggered inside, his hand still groping my ass. My cock was so hard it was painful.

I shut the door and then grunted with surprise when Will pushed me back against the wall. His mouth covered mine and we kissed. It was hungry and urgent with dueling tongues and the occasional clash of teeth.

He tasted strongly of beer and my common sense kicked in. I pushed him back and shook my head. "No, Will."

He took another step away immediately. "Okay. Sorry."

"It's not that I don't want this." I had an undeniable need to reassure him. "But you're drunk and not thinking clearly. When you're sober, you'll remember that you don't want me."

"I'll always want you," he said.

My heart banged against my ribs and warmth flooded my stomach. "Will, I…"

"Fuck," he muttered before leaning against the wall and rubbing at his forehead. "I'm tired."

"Come on, I'll help you to bed." I slid my arm around his waist again. The front door opened directly into his living room, and we walked slowly through it to the narrow hallway on the left.

"Which door is your bedroom?" I asked.

"Last one on the right."

Our hips brushing, we walked to his room and I opened

the door. Will's bedroom was neat and tidy with a queen size bed, two nightstands and a dresser in the far corner. I helped him to the bed and flicked on the lamp, smiling at Will in the warm glow of the light as he collapsed on his back. I took off his shoes and socks as Will fumbled with his belt.

"Let me help," I said.

He squinted up at me. "You get anywhere close to my cock, and I'll have you on your hands and knees and be balls deep in that glorious ass of yours."

I shuddered with pleasure, precum dripping from my cock. I pulled at the front of my jeans, trying to relieve the pressure. Will's gaze moved to my crotch and I shuddered again when he mumbled, "Fuck, I wanna suck you so bad right now."

Before I could do something insane like yank down my pants and present my dick to him like a fucking lollipop, he got his belt unbuckled and his pants unbuttoned. My hands still shaking, I grabbed the legs of his jeans and tugged hard when he lifted his hips. I pulled the jeans down his legs and off his feet, then folded them and set them neatly on top of the dresser. Will sat up and pulled his t-shirt over his head.

He dropped it carelessly on the floor, and I drank in my fill of his smooth chest and perfect eight pack. I was itching to run my fingers over those defined muscles but instead I picked up his t-shirt and set it on top of his jeans. When I turned back to the bed, Will was standing unsteadily by the bed and trying to pull the quilt and sheet back.

I hurried over and helped him, trying not to groan when he lost his balance and had to grab my shoulder to save himself. His hand was hot through my thin shirt and, Christ, did he smell good.

Telling myself not to look, I glanced at his crotch anyway, saliva flooding my mouth when I saw how erect and thick his cock was beneath his briefs. A spot of wetness was at the front and as I watched, Will reached into his briefs and stroked himself. Once…twice… three times.

"Do you want my cock in your ass, Ian?" Will's voice was low and throaty. "Because if that's what you want, I'll give it to you."

"You're drunk, Will." My voice was barely above a whisper.

"I know." His other hand was still on my shoulder and it tightened a little. "I've thought about fucking you way too many times. Even when I believed you were straight."

He studied me, his hand still stroking his cock. "But you're not straight, are you?"

"I don't think so," I said.

He grinned and leaned in to kiss my throat. "I'm sorry I was an asshole to you this afternoon. And I'm really fucking sorry I took advantage of you last week."

I frowned. "You didn't take advantage of me."

"You were upset and not thinking clearly, and I used that to get what I wanted. I'm a fucking asshole."

"I, uh, I'd been wondering what it was like to kiss you for a while. I wanted what happened that day to happen, I promise. You didn't take advantage of me," I said.

He studied me in the dim light. "Stay the night with me."

"I can't. Not when you're drunk," I said. "Get into bed and go to sleep, okay?"

He sighed, his warm breath sending more goosebumps rising across my throat. "Yeah, all right."

He crawled into bed and I pulled the sheet and quilt up. I hesitated and then brushed my hand across his forehead. "Good night, Will."

"Night, Ian. Thank you."

"You're welcome."

Will

I STARED MOROSELY AT MY PHONE AND RUBBED AT MY ACHING skull. I needed to contact him. Needed to apologize for what I'd said and done. I could only hope that Ian didn't go to our principal and demand my resignation after what happened last night. But if he did, I couldn't blame him, nor would I fight it. I'd resign and accept that I'd fucked my life because I couldn't control my dick.

Every part of me wanted to just text Ian – I had his number, all the teachers had contact numbers for each other – but if I were to have any chance of keeping my job, I needed to make a better effort than just a text.

Last night was a bit muddled for me, but I was pretty sure that I'd touched my own damn cock in front of Ian and offered multiple times to fuck him.

I groaned and scooped up the Advil sitting on the table in front of me. I swallowed it down with some water before taking a fortifying sip of coffee. The caffeine and hot liquid bolstered me a bit, and before I could chicken out, I called Ian. My hope it would go to voicemail died when he answered on the second ring.

"Hi, it's Will."

"Hey, you're up early."

I paused with my mug of coffee halfway to my mouth. "Sorry?"

"Considering you probably have one hell of a hangover, you're up early. Unless you're one of those people who never get hangovers?"

"I have a hangover," I said, "but I'm a morning person."

Ian laughed. "Sucks to be you."

"Yeah. Listen, I'm calling to apologize about last night. I'm sorry for what I said and did. It was inappropriate and I have no excuse for it."

"Apology accepted," Ian said.

I choked a bit on my sip of coffee. "I... what?"

"I said apology accepted," Ian replied. "What did you think I would say?"

"I don't know," I admitted.

There was an awkward silence that I hurried to break. "Thanks for the ride home too."

"You're welcome. Do you need a ride to pick up your car?"

"Uh..."

I had planned on texting Tristan later and asking him to take me back to the pub to get my car, but Ian's offer was more appealing.

"I don't live far from you," Ian said, "and my day is open. Your choice though."

"Sure," I said. "Thank you. Can you give me half an hour?"

"Yep. See you soon." He hung up quickly like he thought I might change my mind.

Honestly? He wasn't wrong. I was already regretting my impulse decision. The smart thing to do would be to stay as far away from Ian Smith as I could. So, why wasn't I doing just that?

HALF AN HOUR LATER, IAN WAS PARKED IN MY DRIVEWAY. I climbed into his car, smiling tentatively at him. "Thanks again."

"Don't mention it." He drove down the street toward

the pub.

"So, you live close by?" I said.

He nodded. "Yes. I have a condo in CastleView."

"It looks like a nice complex," I said. "Very clean."

I groaned inwardly as Ian laughed. "Yeah, they keep the grounds looking pretty good. I just rent though. I don't own my condo."

"Oh," I said.

"Lori and I were looking at houses in your neighbourhood a few months ago," Ian said.

"Really?"

"Yes. She was reluctant to buy with me though, so we only looked at a couple of houses before she said she didn't want to look anymore. I thought it was the money thing but it turns out it was because she was fucking Frank and not what I'd call invested in our relationship."

I didn't know what to say to that so I kept my mouth shut. Ian glanced at me. "Sorry, I know I sound bitter, but now that I'm over the initial shock of her cheating on me, I'm glad it's over. We would never have worked out."

"Because you're too different?" I said.

"Because I'm not sure what I want," Ian said.

His honesty both impressed and terrified me. I stared out the passenger window, bile burning the back of my throat. "I'm not the guy to help you clear up your confusion. I'm sorry that last night I acted like I was."

"I know," he said. "Where are you parked?"

We were at the pub and I pointed to an empty lot a block down. "Over there. Blue Ford Escape."

He parked next to my vehicle and I made myself look at him. "Thank you again."

"You're welcome."

I opened the door, pausing when Ian said, "You wanna

grab some breakfast? I know a place that has great hangover cure food."

"Ian, I'm not sure that -"

"As friends," he said. "I know you don't want anything else. But we could be friends, couldn't we?"

I needed to say no. Being friends with someone I wanted this much was impossible. Instead, I said, "Yeah, we can be friends."

"Great, follow me in your car. The diner isn't too far from here."

Ian

"YOU WERE RIGHT," WILL SAID. "THIS IS THE BEST hangover cure food I've ever had."

I ate another slice of bacon. "Right? Rachel stumbled onto this place about nine months ago. It looks like a total dive, but the food is crazy good. I think it's all the grease."

"It's definitely the grease." Will mopped up some egg with his toast. "I'll have to work out an extra hour tomorrow because of this breakfast."

"Totally worth it," I said.

"Yup."

I sipped at my cup of coffee. Unlike the food, the coffee was terrible, but I'd grown used to the burnt beans taste. I studied Will as he cleared the rest of his plate before taking his own cautious sip of coffee.

I laughed again at the look on his face. "Their coffee on the other hand..."

"Tastes like shit," Will said, then took another sip anyway.

"Can I ask you a question?" I said.

He nodded and I pushed my empty plate away and folded my arms across the table. "Have you ever been to Sapphire's?"

"Yes."

"Is it...nice?" Fuck, I sounded stupid.

He studied me over the edge of his coffee cup. "It's one of the nicer gay bars in town but still a meat market."

"There are more gay bars in town than just Sapphire?" I stared at him in surprise.

"Yes. Sapphire is just the one best known by the straights. If you're looking to hide that you're gay, you're better off going to Radiance. It's over on the west end and is much more… discreet."

"I'm not looking to hide anything," I said. My skin prickled in irritation. "I told you before that what I said in the janitor's closet had nothing to do with the gay thing and everything to do with inappropriateness at work."

He rubbed at his forehead. "I know."

"Then stop acting like I'm trying to hide something."

"I apologize," he said stiffly.

Silence descended over us. Will glanced at me. "Why are you asking about gay bars?"

Hoping he wouldn't think less of me, but knowing he probably would, I said, "I'm trying to clear up some of my uncertainty."

Like a little kid, I crossed my fingers under the table. I was secretly hoping that Will would volunteer to help, despite what he'd said earlier. There was an obvious attraction between us. While it was clear that he had strong feelings about a guy being in the closet, maybe my insistence that I didn't want to hide anything, would convince him.

"Rachel suggested I find someone to, uh, show me

some… stuff. She thinks it might help me know whether I'm gay or bi."

"Why are you in such a hurry to put a label on it? You're attracted to men, so on the Kinsey Scale we know you aren't a zero, totally heterosexual. Wherever else you fall is irrelevant right now."

I flushed. "It's not that simple."

"Yes, it is. You're trying to make it into something more than it actually is," Will said.

"Maybe you're right," I said.

"So, what you're really looking for is someone to pop your ass cherry," Will said. He'd affected the perfect *straight bro* dude tone, sounding like a scarily accurate imitation of most of the guys at my old frat house.

I didn't know Will all that well, but I had a feeling he was being purposefully crude. Why, I wasn't sure, but if he thought it would scare me off or change my mind, he was dead wrong.

"Yes," I said, "that's what I'm looking for. You interested in helping me out?"

His face flushed and he swallowed half the cup of coffee with a grimace. "No."

"That's what I thought," I said.

"Going to a bar and picking up some random guy isn't the answer," Will said. "Plus, you just got out of a relationship."

I shrugged. "It's not ideal, but it's a start. And I'm not looking to date someone, so what does it matter that I just ended a relationship? I'm not marrying the guy, Will."

"You're honestly gonna go to pick up a stranger at the bar and let him fuck you in the ass?" Will said.

"Why are you angry?" I said. "I've offered you the chance to do it and you don't want to."

"I'm not angry." Will's face was red and the hand not

holding his coffee mug was curled into a tight fist. "I just think your idea of picking up a stranger at a bar is a dangerous one."

"I'm a good judge of character," I said, "but I see your point. Maybe I'll try a dating app instead."

Will grimaced. "Jesus, that's even worse. You get on that app and announce you're looking for someone to take your cherry, and the weirdos will come out of the woodwork."

I laughed. "Then Sapphire's it is. Thanks for your help, Will."

He glared at me. "I'm not *helping* you. I'm telling you that neither of those options are good."

"I disagree," I said. "Rachel and I have already made plans to go to Sapphire's tonight and -"

"Tonight?" Will's eyes nearly bugged out of his head. "You're going tonight?"

"We are," I said.

"Two weeks ago, you were living with a woman and happily fucking her night after night," Will said. "Now suddenly you're acting gayer than a bucket of sequins and looking to have sex with some random dude. This isn't you, Ian. You don't think that maybe you need to take a step back and ask yourself if you're not having some kind of breakdown because your long-term relationship ended?"

"Lori and I weren't fucking night after night," I said. "In fact, we hadn't fucked in months. And the final straw for her leaving was me asking her to fuck my ass with a strap-on. So, maybe try looking down from that high horse you've climbed up onto, and consider that you don't know my life at all before you start judging me."

Will stared at me in mute surprise, but anger was bubbling out of me like hot lava, and I couldn't stop it. "And you know what? I'd appreciate it if you'd stop making me feel like this is nothing more than a mental breakdown. I already have Lori in my head telling me that I'm sick and need help. I don't need you in there too."

I grabbed the bill from the table and slid out of the booth. "Thanks for your advice, Will, but I don't think we should be friends. I'll see you on Monday."

"Ian, wait, I didn't mean…"

I ignored him and walked to the front to pay our bill. My face was hot, and my stomach was churning, and I was seriously pissed. And not knowing if I was pissed because Will had basically just accused me of being crazy, or because he'd turned down my offer to fuck me, was making me even angrier.

I smiled thinly at the cashier, shoved my wallet into my back pocket, and walked out of the diner.

CHAPTER 6

WILL

I sipped at my drink and studied the bar and the area beyond it. Sapphire's was crowded as usual, and my unease deepened instead of lessening when I couldn't find Ian. I wanted to believe that what I'd said to him this morning had gotten through to him, but that nagging, niggling part of me that said I was wrong, wouldn't let go. It was early in the night, but maybe he'd found someone quickly and they'd already left.

I grimaced and took another sip of my soda water. That was most likely the case. There were dozens of guys here who'd be willing to fuck Ian. The fact that he was looking for no commitment made that number skyrocket.

The bass from the dance floor thumped and thumped. The sound made my teeth vibrate. It was a damn good job my headache had gone away, or I'd be in agony right now. I weaved my way through the crowds, looking for Ian with a growing worry that I couldn't conceal. Maybe I should try texting him.

Like he doesn't have your number blocked, buddy. He said he didn't want to be friends, remember?

I remembered, but we were still co-workers. He wouldn't block my number. I reached into my pocket for my phone, scowling when someone bumped into me and half my drink spilled on the already-sticky floor.

"Oh my gosh, I'm so sorry."

The voice was weirdly familiar. I turned, my heart kicking up a notch when I saw Ian's friend Rachel.

"Rachel! Hey, uh, do you remember me from last night? I'm Will. I work with Ian."

"Hey, Will." She grinned at me. "Of course, I remember you. How's it going?"

"Good," I said.

"Sorry I spilled your drink," she said. "Can I buy you another one?"

"It's fine, it's just soda water," I said.

"Tabitha!" Rachel waved at someone and a small blonde joined us. "Tabs this is Will. He works with Ian."

"Nice to meet you!" Tabitha shouted over the blaring music.

"You too." I shook her hand before glancing at Rachel. "Ian's here, right?"

She nodded and relief swept through me. "Great, good. Do you know where he is?"

She pointed to the dance floor before sipping at her drink. "Dancing."

I scanned the dance floor, jealousy flooding through me when I saw a man behind Ian, holding his hips and grinding up against his ass. The guy whispered something into Ian's ear and a weird look crossed Ian's face. Apprehension and nervousness, mixed with the tiniest bit of *what the fuck am I doing?*

My back prickled and I practically shoved my drink at Rachel. "Could you hold this for me?"

"Sure." She took my drink, and I headed to the dance floor as the song ended and another began. This one was soft and slow, and as the men on the dance floor broke into couples, I pushed my way past them toward Ian.

The man he was with was holding his hand and trying to pull him into his arms. Ian shook his head, and anger burned in my belly when the man refused to let go of his hand. I was close enough now that I heard the man say, "C'mon, just one dance. Don't be a fucking tease."

"He's not interested, asshole," I growled.

Ian glanced behind him, his eyes widening. "Will? What are you doing here?"

"Get lost," the man said.

I took Ian's free hand and stared steadily at the man. "You get lost. Now."

I wasn't much for physical intimidation or fighting, but the guy being possessive over Ian, maybe thinking that he'd be the one to fuck Ian, was riling me up to the point where I was puffing out my chest like a honey badger ready to go to battle.

The guy rolled his eyes and dropped Ian's hand. "Whatever. He's too much of a twink for me anyway."

He pushed his way past the dancers. Ian didn't object when I put my arm around his waist and pulled him in close. In fact, he draped his arms over my shoulders and started swaying to the music. "Did that guy seriously just call me a twink? I'll admit I don't know a lot about the gay culture, but I'm pretty sure I'm not a twink. Am I?"

His earnest look of confusion made me laugh despite the jealousy and fury still raging in my belly. "No, you're not. An otter, maybe."

"An otter? What's an otter?"

"It's supposed to be funny, you're not really an otter either…just, never mind.'

"So, what are you doing here?" Ian's warm breath washed over my face. I couldn't smell any alcohol, thank God, but I still had to ask.

"How much have you had to drink?"

He frowned. "I'm not drinking tonight. I need to be clear-headed when I'm making this type of choice."

My hands tightened on his hips. "So, you're still planning on going through with this."

"Yes," Ian said. "Why are you here?"

"I'm sorry I made you feel bad earlier. Lori is wrong. There's nothing sick about you."

"You came out to Sapphire's tonight to apologize?" Ian said. "Why not just text me?"

I didn't reply and Ian pressed his mouth to my ear. My cock immediately hardened, and I heard Ian's light groan when it pressed against his hip. "Why are you really here, Will?"

"To change your mind about going through with this."

"I appreciate your tenacity, but there's no changing my mind." Ian leaned back and grinned at me. "You wanna help me pick out someone?"

"Jesus Christ, no," I said. "I want you to realize this is dangerous and stupid and go the fuck home."

"Not gonna happen," Ian said. "I'm getting my cherry popped tonight, Will."

"See, you thinking it's all about being fucked in your ass, is the problem," I said.

"What do you mean." Ian shifted positions, and my throat went dry when our cocks rubbed against each other.

Ian bit at his bottom lip. "Fuck, your cock is so hard."

"Stop distracting me." I squeezed his hips again and tried not to remember how good his lips tasted as I put a little space between our bodies. "It's not all about fucking, Ian. You don't have to have sex the very first time you're with a guy."

"I'm sure they'll want to. It's fine with me," Ian said carelessly.

I could feel a muscle ticking in my jaw. Irritated by how nonchalant he was being, I reached down and gripped one firm ass cheek, squeezing hard while I ground my cock against his. "You don't know that, Ian. You've already admitted that you don't know exactly what you want. Isn't that right?"

Ian moaned into my ear, his hands digging into my upper back. "Yes," he said, "but I don't see much way around it."

"Find someone who's willing to go slow," I said. "Who won't rush to fuck you tonight. Someone who's been a guy's first before."

"Have you been a guy's first before?" Ian said.

I hesitated before nodding. "Yeah."

"Sounds like I've found my guy then."

"I can't."

He studied me, his eyes full of honest confusion. "Why not, though? Is it that you think I'll want a relationship? I promise I won't. I'm not interested in a relationship with a co-worker, not after what I just went through with Lori. I won't ask you for more than sex, and even then, once we've done it, we can be just friends after that or even," he paused and something that looked like regret flashed in his eyes, "go back to the way things were between us."

"It'll make things complicated at work," I said.

"No, it won't. We're both adults and we both know what

this is. If we treat it like a random hook up, things don't have to get awkward, right?"

I didn't answer and Ian chewed at his bottom lip in that endearing way he had before hesitantly pressing a kiss below my ear. "You want me, Will. I want you. Why can't we have what we both want? No commitment, no deeper feelings. Just you teaching me how good we can make each other feel."

My defenses were lowering, which was the worst possible response, but, fuck, I wanted Ian. I'd wanted him for a very long time. It was ironic that he thought I was hesitating because I didn't want a relationship with him, when in fact I wanted that more than anything. But I couldn't tell him my true feelings. He'd made it perfectly clear he wasn't inter- ested in dating me. With the way Lori was spreading shit about him at work, I couldn't blame him.

Still, I had to say no. I was setting myself up for pain and I wasn't a sadist. Letting my cock make the decision was stupid. I opened my mouth to tell him no but couldn't spit it out. An image of Ian's face when that guy had whispered in his ear, the look of anxiety he couldn't hide, kept flickering through my head. He was saying all the right things, but Ian was nervous about doing this. Very nervous. And what kind of asshole did it make me to just let him go off with someone who didn't know what the fuck they were doing, when I was the perfect man for the job?

So, it has nothing to do with your jealousy over someone else being Ian's first?

I ignored my inner voice and studied Ian's face. He was waiting patiently as we stood in the middle of the dance floor, our bodies barely swaying to the music, my hand still grip- ping his ass and our hard cocks pressed together.

"I'll do it," I said.

Ian's body relaxed against mine and relief flooded his face. "Yeah?"

"Yes. C'mon, let's go back to my place." I took his hand and led him off the dance floor.

IAN

"YOU WANT SOMETHING TO DRINK?" WILL SAID. "I HAVE water or juice. There might be a couple sodas in -"

"I'm not thirsty." I took Will's hand, leading him to the bedroom, despite it being his house and not mine.

"Ian, are you positive this is what you want?" Will turned the bedside lamp on, his face pensive and his gaze uncertain.

"I am," I said. "Do you want this?"

He ran a hand through his dark hair. "You know I do."

"Then we're all good."

"Yeah. If at any time you want to stop, just say so, okay?"

I grinned at him. "Do I need a safe word?"

"Jesus Christ, no, you don't need a safe word. I'm not into BDSM or -"

"Will, I'm joking. Relax," I said.

Will blew his breath out in a harsh rush. "Joking, right."

"Hey, look at this, would you?" I held my phone out to him. Will took my phone, studying the screen for a few minutes before looking at me. "Your medical records? We're not having sex tonight, Ian."

"I know," I said. "But I still thought it would be good for you to see my results. My last tests were just last month."

"You got tested even though you were in a relationship?" Will said.

I shrugged. "Lori insisted we both get tested on a regular

basis. I just thought it was a weird quirk of hers, or a misplaced lack of trust, which is super fucking ironic considering she was the one sleeping around. Anyway, Lori and I haven't had sex in over two months, so those results are still accurate."

Will nodded before pulling out his phone and typing for a few minutes. He handed it over. "These are mine. Tested six months ago, haven't been with anyone in nine months."

"Jesus, why not?" I said.

He just shrugged, but his gaze cut away from mine. "A lot on my plate right now with work and other stuff."

I handed Will his phone and took mine from him. "Okay, so we're good for no condoms then?"

"We're not having sex tonight," he reminded me.

"But when we do…"

"No condom is fine with me. As long as you haven't slept with anyone between now and then," Will said.

"I'm not going to." I was feeling a little hurt by what he said but tried to shake it off. "The deal was that you would be my first, remember?"

He nodded. "Yeah."

"Great, then let's get started," I said.

He hesitated briefly before turning down the quilt and the sheet. "Get undressed."

Feeling awkward, I said, "Yeah, you're gonna have to work a little harder than that to see me naked, buddy."

A small smile crossed Will's face. "Is that right?"

"Uh-huh." I crossed my arms over my chest. "I don't know what you've heard about me, but I don't put out just like that."

"You sure? I did catch you making out with Patty in the staff room," Will said.

"Ugh, don't remind me," I said. "She tasted like Cheetos and her tongue was… large."

Will laughed, and I grinned at him. "Thanks for rescuing me, by the way."

"You're welcome." He moved closer and reached out to snag my belt loop. He pulled me forward and kissed my neck. I groaned, and Will nipped my jaw before kissing just below my ear. "You're so fucking hot, Ian."

"See," I moaned when he slid his hand under my shirt and stroked my stomach, "this is how you get me naked. I respond very well to flattery."

His soft chuckle in my ear made my dick turn to stone. "Good to know."

He tugged off my shirt and kissed a path across my chest. I cupped the back of his skull, letting my head fall back and closing my eyes. His firm lips and lightly callused fingertips were a different sensation that I was rapidly becoming addicted to. When he sucked on one flat nipple, my back arched, and I made an unintelligible sound of need.

He teased my nipple until I was gasping and rubbing my cock against him. He lifted his head and grinned at me. "Someone's got sensitive nips, huh?"

"I had no fucking idea," I gasped out. "I've never had them sucked on before."

"Jesus," he said, "you've really been dating the wrong women."

"Yeah," I moaned as his fingers unbuckled my belt and then unbuttoned my jeans, "I think you might be right."

He slipped his hand inside my underwear and his warm fingers wrapped around my cock. I cried out, my hips jerking and my hands gripping his t-shirt. We kissed hungrily, our tongues teasing each other's while Will rubbed my cock with slow firm strokes.

I pulled away, sucking in breath and tugging his hand out of my pants.

"Ian? Am I moving too fast?" Will said.

I shook my head. "No, but you keep doing that and I'm gonna cum in my fucking underwear again."

He laughed. "We can't have that. Get undressed."

"You first," I said with a small grin.

He rolled his eyes but pulled off his t-shirt. I soaked in the sight of his perfect chest and abdomen, a slow burn of excitement flaming to life in my stomach. I took off my shoes and socks as Will did the same, and then stripped off my shirt as Will slid his jeans down his legs. He stepped out of them and I took a minute to stare at his legs. His thighs and calves were heavily muscled – no surprise there, I'd seen him on leg day at the gym – and covered in a light layer of dark hair.

The same shade of dark hair arrowed down from his navel and disappeared under the waistband of his briefs. Precum dripped from my cock as I stared at the bulge behind Will's underwear.

"Ian?" Will was staring at me with his hands hovering at the waistband of his briefs. "If you've changed your mind, that's fine. We can stop."

"I haven't changed my mind," I said. "I'm just… admiring."

He grinned and, with a quick tug, slipped his briefs down his legs and stepped out of them. "Admire away."

"Fuck," I said. "That's um… you've got a really nice dick."

I wasn't blowing smoke up his ass about it. Will did have a beautiful cock. It wasn't as long as mine, but it was deliciously thick. I studied his neatly groomed patch of dark hair at the base, the thick veins running through the shaft and the round blunt head. The head was dark red and already it was slick with precum.

I sounded like a fucking idiot, but Will's grin widened. "Thank you. Take off the rest of your clothes, Ian."

I fumbled briefly with the zipper of my jeans before shoving them and my underwear down my legs.

Will gave my dick his own admiring glance before taking my hand and leading me to the bed. Feeling a little self-conscious, I laid down on my side on the bed. My cock was so hard it stood straight up, the head brushing against my flat abdomen.

Will faced me on his side, and I moaned when our cocks brushed against each other. He leaned in and kissed me again. I lost myself in his taste and the intoxicating feel of his tongue in my mouth.

He leaned back, studying me intently. "Ian, I need you to listen to me, all right?"

I nodded, trying to focus on something other than how good of a kisser he was. "All right."

"Let's forget about your ass right now. That's not the end zone. There are plenty of amazing things we can do along the way. When we get there, and we will, if you don't like it, that doesn't mean you're not into guys. It just means you're not into ass play. There are plenty of gay men who have never had anal sex, and there's nothing wrong with that either. How you feel about ass play isn't indicative of your sexuality. Do you understand?"

"Yeah, I do."

"Good. Tonight's going to be incredible, Ian. I promise," Will said.

When he took both of our cocks in his hand and rubbed up and down, I groaned into his mouth and tried not to embarrass myself by cumming right there. The pressure of

Will's hand, the slick glide of his cock against mine, was a heady mix of pleasure and new sensation.

He rubbed harder, his tongue teasing mine as I ran my hands tentatively over his chest. My finger brushed his flat nipple and his cock twitched against mine. I smiled at him. "Yours are sensitive too."

"Yeah," he gasped before kissing down my neck. He was still rubbing us together and when he nipped at the base of my neck, I cried out, my hands digging into his hard chest.

"Fuck, Will, I'm gonna cum," I groaned.

"We can't have that." He released both of us, ignoring my moan of dismay. "At least not yet anyway."

"I disagree." I cupped the back of Will's head, arching when he kissed down my chest.

He traced my abs with his tongue. I moaned and twisted, my fingers digging into his scalp. His chin brushed the head of my dick, and I cried out, my hips bucking. Will kissed my v-line, his fingers running over the short blond hair at the base of my dick.

"You doing okay?" His warm breath on my skin was driving me crazy.

"Yeah," I groaned.

"You sure?"

I stared down at him. "Yes. Are you?" I was suddenly worried that he was getting cold feet.

"I am, but I want to make sure you still want this."

"Why wouldn't I?" I said.

His smile was half amusement and half exasperation. "Oh, I don't know. Maybe because you've never had a guy suck your dick before?"

"That's true, but I can tell you with one hundred percent confidence that I've spent a lot of nights imagining it and watching it on porn."

"Is that right?" Will nibbled on my hip bone, his hand sliding around the base of my dick and giving it a light squeeze.

"Yeah," I groaned.

"Anyone in particular you pictured sucking your glorious dick?" Will said.

"Carter Anderson."

He paused in licking a path below my belly button. "Who?"

"Guy at university." I pumped my hips, trying to get Will to rub my cock again.

"If you were into guys in university, why didn't you experiment then?"

"Not guys. Guy," I said. "Carter specifically. I thought it was just a weird brain blip until..."

"Until?" Will said.

I ran my fingers through his hair. "You."

He stared up at me, his fingers tightening around my cock. "Me."

"Yes. I've been attracted to you since you started at the school. I've had more than one fantasy of you sucking on my cock and, um, vice versa."

"Well," Will's grin was adorably cheesy, "time to make that fantasy a reality."

His mouth slid over the head of my cock and he sucked firmly. I cried out, my entire body tensing as an incredible wave of pleasure washed over me. I stared down at Will, not wanting to miss a single moment of the experience.

It was as good as I'd imagined. The way Will looked with his lips sliding up and down my dick, the exquisite suction of his hot wet mouth, the delicious slide of his tongue across my sensitive shaft, made my balls tighten and the base of my spine tingle. When he reached between my legs and pressed lightly on my taint, I was a fucking goner.

"Cumming," I managed to croak out. "Will, I'm…"

The pleasure consumed me. Will's lips tightened around my dick and I came into his mouth harder than I'd ever cum in my damn life. I clutched at his hair, my hips jerking and twisting and my back arching as Will swallowed every last drop.

I collapsed on the bed, gasping for air as Will sat up. He kneeled beside me and took his dick in his hand. He stroked hard, staring down at my body as he rubbed and pinched his flat nipples with his other hand.

I knew I should be giving him oral sex, or at the very least, a hand job, but my body was still shaking. I was weak and a little disconcerted by the fact that I'd just had the best orgasm of my life.

I shook off the fog and reached for Will, but he made a hoarse cry of pleasure and came all over my stomach. He rubbed hard, shooting his load across my stomach and chest until I was covered in his cum. I stared at the ropes of liquid crisscrossing my flesh, surprised by how much I liked being covered in Will's seed.

Will sank back on his heels on the bed and stared at me.

Embarrassment and regret seeped into my bones. Christ, I had made a real mess of that. I'd cum in less than five minutes and I hadn't done a thing for Will. My first time with a guy and I'd fucked up so badly, I knew without a doubt that Will would never invite me to his bed again.

Nausea churned in my stomach at the thought. Maybe I could convince him to give me another shot. Maybe I could convince him that I wasn't a selfish lover.

Maybe you are selfish. You didn't do it for Lori in bed

either, remember? Maybe you just suck in bed in general – for guys and for women.

Fuck me sideways. Was I terrible at sex?

"Stay there for a minute." Will slid off the bed and went into the adjoined bathroom. He returned with a warm and wet washcloth and carefully and methodically cleaned his cum off my skin.

"Thanks," I said.

He nodded and returned to the bathroom. I stared at the ceiling. I probably should get dressed, right? I didn't expect to spend the night in Will's bed, it wasn't that kind of relationship, but if I was going to convince him that I wasn't selfish in bed, I would need a round two. It was still relatively early and just thinking about what Will had done to me was making my cock stir. I was a little surprised by that. I'd never had what you would call a quick recovery time. But apparently, my dick was ready to prove to Will that I was a real goddamn stud in bed.

The pocket of Will's jeans lit up and I could hear the soft chime of his phone. When he returned, I said, "Someone texted you."

Will studied me. "You okay?"

"Yeah, uh, it was good. Sorry, I nutted off so quick." My face was hot, and yeah, that was definitely regret on Will's face.

Will fished in his jeans for his phone. He glanced at the screen and typed quickly before staring at me. "I have to go."

"What? I – no, right, yeah, okay, I understand," I said even though I really didn't. I climbed out of bed and reached for my clothes. We dressed silently, neither of us looking at each other. Fuck, could this be any more awkward?

"Sorry," Will finally said. "I have a friend who made a bad decision. I need to go pick him up."

"Do you want me to come with you?" I said.

"No, I'm good." Will was walking out of his bedroom and I had no choice but to follow him.

"I don't mind," I said. "Maybe it's better if we both go in case there's trouble or -"

"I don't need your help," Will snapped. He closed his eyes and rubbed at the bridge of his nose. "Sorry, I'm being an asshole. I appreciate the offer, but it's better if I go alone."

"Sure, okay." I shoved my feet into my shoes and grabbed my jacket. I opened the front door, expecting Will to follow me out. When he only stood there, I flushed and said, "See you on Monday."

His phone buzzed and he made a half-hearted wave at me before typing rapidly. Feeling stupid and embarrassed, I shut the door and practically ran to my car.

CHAPTER 7

WILL

"You okay?" I stared worriedly at Tristan when he opened the door and sat in the passenger seat. He slammed the door shut and rubbed at his forehead. The smell of whiskey and weed was overpowering and I opened my window and his.

"Christ, you stink," I said. "Since when did you start smoking weed?"

"I haven't," Tristan said. "Jared smokes it. Can we go?"

"Seatbelt," I said.

Tristan put on his seatbelt and I pulled out into the street. I headed toward Tristan's house. "You wanna talk about it?"

"What's there to say? I had too much to drink and went home with a guy I shouldn't have."

"What did he do to you?" My body tensed and I could feel my face reddening.

Tristan glanced at me. "Calm down, Will. I outweigh Jared by sixty pounds and I'm half a foot taller. He didn't do anything to me I didn't want him to do."

I relaxed a little. "Tell me what happened."

"I don't want to talk about it."

"Bullshit," I said. "If you didn't want to talk, you would have called an Uber to pick up your drunk ass. Talk, Tristan."

Tristan rubbed at his forehead. "We met at the Gem, had a few drinks, and he invited me back to his place. The sex was... fine."

"Fine," I said.

"Yes," Tristan said. "Fine. He smoked some weed, we played some video games, and then he brought out some blow and asked me to do a line with him."

"Jesus Christ," I stopped at a red light and stared at Tristan. "Tell me you didn't."

"I didn't." Tristan said. "He did a couple lines and then wanted to fuck again, but he couldn't get it up."

"Yeah, because he was fucked up on coke," I said.

"He got pissy, said it was because I couldn't suck his cock well enough. I called him an addict and left. Sat on his front step and texted you for a ride home."

"Is he an addict?" I said.

"How the fuck would I know?" Tristan said. "I just met him tonight."

He rubbed at his forehead again. The light turned green and I stepped on the gas. "Okay, so I'm not getting what the problem was. Other than you having not so great sex with a dickhead."

"I almost tried some of the coke." Tristan stared out the passenger window.

My stomach clenched, and I gripped the steering wheel until my knuckles went white. I wanted to immediately start yelling, mostly due to sheer panic, but I kept my cool. I'd been friends with Tristan for a long time and I knew perfectly well that if I got angry and started yelling, he'd shut down.

"Why?" I said, pleased at how nonjudgmental I sounded.

"I don't know." Tristan sighed. "Because I was bored, because I figured what's the big deal, because I'm tired of…"

"Tired of what?" I said.

He still refused to look at me. "Tired of feeling like I'm broken."

"You're not broken." I reached over and squeezed his arm. "Don't let your dad get in your head again. You were dying at his company, Tristan. Taking over the family business would have been the thing that *did* break you."

"I'm his only kid. Walking away like I did means that the business he worked so hard to build dies with him. What kind of son does that to his own father?"

"No, it doesn't," I said. "He can sell the business to someone else when he retires. It won't shut down completely."

"He'd rather shut it down than let someone outside of the family take over," Tristan said.

"That's his choice to make," I said. "It has nothing to do with you."

"It has everything to do with me," Tristan said. "You know how much he hates that I'm a mechanic. He can't even look me in the eye when we're together now."

"Look, your dad always was an asshole," I said, "even when you were wearing a three-piece suit and working under his fucking thumb every single day, he wasn't happy. You've loved cars since we were kids, Tristan. Being a mechanic makes you happy. You're allowed to live your life free from your father's demands. You're not a little kid anymore."

"He's disappointed in me," Tristan said.

"So what? Let him be fucking disappointed. It doesn't mean that you're a fuck up."

"You don't understand. Your dad is proud of you. He thinks everything you do is amazing," Tristan said.

I pulled into the parking lot of Tristan's apartment building and killed the engine. I twisted in my seat to face him. "Do you really want the approval of a guy who thinks that blue collar jobs are some sort of failure? I know you love your dad, but he's the one who's broken inside, not you."

Tristan finally looked at me. He took a deep breath and nodded. "Yeah, okay. Thanks, Will. I hope I didn't fuck up your night."

"You didn't," I said. "Quiet night in." I wasn't about to tell him that he'd interrupted my night with the man of my fucking dreams. He'd never forgive himself.

You should have let Ian come with you.

I couldn't. Tristan would have been embarrassed, and I wouldn't do that to my best friend.

Then you should have asked him to stay at your place while you were gone.

I stared at my hands that were clenched around the steering wheel again. Maybe I should have, but I'd been worried about Tristan and not thinking straight. My worry had made me short-tempered with Ian.

Was it just that? Or was it the look on Ian's face after you came all over him. Ian can't hide a thing on that gorgeous face of his, can he? Although I'm not sure if it was the shame or the regret that was more apparent. What do you think?

I ignored my inner voice even though it wasn't wrong in the least. It was no big deal anyway. Ian wanted to know what it was like to be with a guy. I gave him a taste of it, he discovered it wasn't for him. I knew that was a possibility. It wasn't Ian's fault that he wasn't into it the way he thought he might be.

Or maybe he's just not into you *the way he thought he would be.*

Oh, look, my knuckles were white again. I forced myself to relax my grip around the steering wheel and acknowledge what inner me was saying. Yes, it could be entirely possible that sex with me wasn't what Ian hoped it would be. It was also possible that he'd be out next weekend, searching for a different guy to experiment with. I needed to accept it and forget all about Ian Smith and his perfect dick.

IAN

"BABE, WE HAVE ALL DONE THE WALK OF SHAME," RACHEL handed me an iced tea, "it's nothing to be embarrassed about."

"It was more like the sprint of shame," I said. I gulped back some iced tea before leaning my head against the back of the couch. "Fuck, I'm such an idiot."

"No, you're not." Rachel was sprawled out on the other end of the couch. "Will is a loser for doing the fake 'friend needs help' text."

"Wait, what?" I sat up straight. "You think he was faking needing to leave last night?"

"Oh, my sweet summer child," Rachel said. "Of course it was fake. There's never a friend who needs help."

"It seemed pretty real to me."

"Did you actually see him leave the house? Get in his car and drive away?" Rachel said.

"No," I admitted.

"There you go." Rachel drank some of her water.

I sank back in the couch, depression washing over me. "Holy fuck, he faked me out."

"Sorry, Ian." Rachel reached over and patted my hand. "He's an asshole."

"I shouldn't be surprised," I said. "I lasted less than five fucking minutes. Of course he lost interest."

"Hey, stop it." Rachel frowned at me. "This is not your fault. One, it was your first time with a guy, so yeah, you're gonna be a little excited about it. And two, if the guy runs after one accidental quick nut, then you don't want to be with him anyway. We can find someone better out there for you. If you're still interested, that is?"

"I am," I said. I ignored the way my stomach tensed up. I *was* still interested. It was just that I was still interested in Will, which was ridiculous because the guy lied to me.

"Cool. You want to try Sapphire's again, or a dating app this time?" Rachel said.

"Sapphire's," I said. "I really didn't give it much of a chance, right?"

"True. Friday at ten? I can see if Tabs wants to go with us again."

"Sure," I said, ignoring the way my stomach felt like it was bobbing along in turbulent waters. "Friday at ten."

"IAN, CAN I SPEAK TO YOU FOR A MINUTE?"

I turned around and backtracked to the door of the school's main office. Joe was standing in the doorway and I made myself smile at our affable principal. "Sure."

I followed him into his office. He shut the door and motioned for me to take a seat in one of the leather chairs across from his desk. I sank into the soft leather as Joe took his chair. He closed his laptop and folded his hands across his immaculately clean desk.

I kept a pleasant look on my face, but truthfully, I was annoyed and tired and already feeling impatient. It was after four on Friday and I'd been on my way out the door. I was ready to be away from the damn school for a few days. Normally, I loved my job, but that was before I had to spend an entire week avoiding Will. I hadn't stepped foot in the staff room all week, I limited my time to the gym and my tiny office, and as soon as the bell rang at the end of the day, I ran straight to my car like a scared little kid.

I hadn't planned to avoid him, but Monday morning, as I was staring at the front door of the school and contemplating the possibility of quitting and finding a new job in a different school, I realized avoiding him was a necessity. Not just because of my embarrassment over what happened Friday night, but because my attraction to him wouldn't go away if I saw him every goddamn day. Hell, just thinking about his hot mouth, and the way he'd sucked me off, made me hard as stone. If I actually saw him, who knew what the hell would happen.

So, I'd spent the entire week skulking around the school, praying and hoping I didn't run into him. My brain and my dick needed time to forget what he looked like naked.

I realized that Joe was studying me with a somber look on his face and I straightened in the chair, unease nipping at my gut. What was going on?

"What's wrong, Joe?" I asked.

"I wanted to speak with you about some unpleasant rumours that have been circulating around the school this week among teachers and students."

His slight accent on the word students made my stomach

plummet to the floor. Had someone seen Will and me at Sapphire's last Friday?

Who cares if they did? It's not a fucking crime to be gay.

I took a deep breath. "I'm not sure what you've heard, but Lori and I are no longer together. What I did last Friday with _"

"I'm aware you and Lori have," Joe paused, looking deeply uncomfortable, "broken up. I'm also aware that it was not an amicable breakup. While I don't know the entire story, spreading these types of rumours about Lori is unprofessional and unacceptable. As you can imagine, her reputation with her students has taken an enormous hit, and I've had multiple parents calling with complaints about inappropriate conduct at the school."

"Joe, I have no idea what you're talking about," I said.

He frowned. "There's no point in denying it. You and Will were the only ones who witnessed Lori and Frank's indiscretion in her classroom. Lori and Frank certainly didn't spread the rumours about Lori so naturally -"

"Naturally, you assume it's me because Lori was cheating on me with Frank," I said.

"Yes," Joe said bluntly. "Lori told me how upset you were, and she told me you attacked Frank. You're lucky he didn't have you arrested for assault."

I leaned forward. "I didn't say a word to anyone about Lori and Frank having sex in her classroom."

"Lori assures me that contrary to the rumours you started, she and Frank were not having sex," Joe said. "It was kissing and a bit of..." his face turned a deep red, and I would have felt sorry for him if I wasn't so pissed off, "groping."

"It wasn't me," I said. "I don't appreciate you pulling me into your office to accuse me of something I didn't do. Especially without proof."

"Are you telling me that it was Will who started the rumour at the school?"

"Of course not," I said. I actually sounded like I believed that. "But what I am telling you is that it wasn't me either."

Joe sighed deeply, rubbing at his bald head before sitting back in his chair. "I don't know what to tell you, Ian. Lori insists that it's you. Insists that you're getting back at her for breaking up with you. It's a real goddamn mess."

"Look, I get it, okay? But I'm not taking the blame for something I didn't do."

Joe sighed again. "Someone spray painted the word whore on Lori's car just after lunch."

"Jesus," I said. "Joe, you can't honestly think that was me?"

"I don't," he said. "Hell, for all I know, it could be students who did it. She's been having a hell of a time keeping control in her classroom right now. She says the students keep giggling and talking behind her back. One of them drew a crude drawing of her and Frank on the white-board when she was out of the room. Parents are asking me to suspend her and Frank without pay for a week, if not outright fire them both."

Despite what Lori had said to me, despite the fact that she'd cheated on me, I still felt sorry for her. No one deserved that kind of treatment, and I couldn't believe that Will had started all of this. Why the hell would he tell everyone about Lori and Frank? He had to have known Lori would assume it was me.

Oh, I dunno. Maybe because you coerced him into spending the night with you where you didn't do one damn thing but lie there and let him suck your dick. Or maybe it's because you've avoided him for an entire week like you're ashamed of what the two of you did together.

The knot in my stomach tightened excruciatingly. Okay, so maybe avoiding him did give Will the impression that I was embarrassed about what happened between us, but that didn't give him the right to talk shit about Lori or cost her her damn job.

"Ian?" Joe said. "Lori and Frank want you fired for -"

"I didn't do it!" I snapped. "You can't fire me for something you have no proof of, Joe. If you even try, I'll go to the -"

Joe held up his hand. "Hold on, I'm not firing you. I told them the same thing."

"But you came into this conversation believing that I did it," I said. "You still think I did."

He shook his head wearily. "I'm sorry. I shouldn't have – that is, it was stupid of me to think you would do this. But Lori made a very compelling argument for why it was you and, to be fair, the spurned lover getting revenge is well known for a reason."

I barked out harsh laughter. "I don't give a fuck that Lori and I aren't together, Joe. In fact, I'm glad we aren't. She did me a favour by dumping me."

"Right," he said. He straightened the already perfectly straight inbox on the corner of his desk. "I apologize for approaching this the way I did. I should have asked you for your side of the story before accusing you."

"Thanks for the apology," I said. "If we're done, I'd like to go. I have plans for tonight."

My plan to go to Sapphire's with Rachel was still a go, but first... I was stopping by Will Matthews house and letting him know exactly what a huge dickhead he was.

CHAPTER 8

WILL

I stared at the leftovers on the counter before popping them in the microwave. I had no desire to eat. My appetite had disappeared by Tuesday when I realized that, yes, Ian really was avoiding me.

But starving myself wouldn't accomplish anything, and besides, what did I expect? I'd basically kicked him out of my house Friday night with barely an explanation. I leaned against the counter and stared out the window above the sink. I should have forced Ian to talk to me this week, should have at the very least told him that Tristan was my best friend and that's why I'd ditched Ian. But knowing Ian's new desire to keep his personal life separate from work – and I couldn't blame him for that – it didn't feel right to corner him in his office or some quiet part of the school and try to explain.

You could have texted or called, asshole.

I studied the bird sitting on the fence, its bright yellow feathers catching the light of the evening sun. Yeah, I could have. Almost did. Until I realized that there wasn't any point beyond trying to make myself feel better for being an asshole. The look of regret and shame on Ian's face after we'd both cum, kept inserting itself into my brain at random times, and each time it brought on my own feelings of regret and shame. Ian was confused, and I'd used that confusion for my own selfish reasons.

The microwave beeped, and I popped the leftovers out and stirred them before sticking them back in for another few minutes. My decision to forget what happened between Ian and me wasn't going very smoothly. Even though I'd spent the entire week basically hiding out in my classroom. Hell, I'd only gone to the staff room when I was absolutely sure Ian was teaching a class.

Ian and I couldn't avoid each other forever, not in a school as small as ours, but right now, everything was still too raw and –

The doorbell rang and I glanced at the clock over the stove before leaving the kitchen. I slowed to a stop as I walked down the hallway, staring in surprise at Ian through the window in the door. For a moment, I considered just turning around and walking away, but then Ian said, "Open the door, Will."

I forced my wooden legs to carry me forward, opening the door and stepping back when Ian barged in past me. He slammed the door shut and glared at me. "That was a really shitty thing for you to do."

"Look, I know, okay?" I said. "But Tristan is my best friend and he needed me to pick him up. I shouldn't have -"

Ian made a sound of exasperation. "Oh, for fuck's sake, Will, I'm not talking about Friday night. Don't play dumb."

I stared cautiously at him. Ian was one of the most level-headed and easy-going teachers at the school, and Angry Ian wasn't someone I'd seen before. I wondered what kind of guy it made me, to want to take Angry Ian to my bed and make him suck my dick. A first-rate asshole, probably. But holy fuck, a pissed-off Ian was kind of hot.

"I don't know what you're talking about, Ian," I said.

Ian jabbed his hand through his blond hair, making it stick up at odd angles. "Lori! I'm talking about Lori and Frank."

"What about them?" I said.

"Jesus," he said, "really, Will? You told half the goddamn school about Lori and Frank fucking in her classroom. The teachers are gossiping about her, she's lost control of her students, someone wrote whore on her car in spray paint, and the parents want her fucking fired! Does that make you feel good about yourself, Will? Does it?"

"I didn't do or say -"

"You know, it's a really shitty thing for you to take your anger with me out on Lori. I get that you knew Lori would assume it was me and that I'd be in trouble with Joe for it, and guess what? Your plan worked. But there's a little thing called proof that's required, Will, and without it, Joe can't do a fucking thing to me. But Lori's reputation is ruined and -"

"Hey, stop! Slow down for a second," I said. "I didn't do any of that, Ian."

Thick silence filled the hallway. From the kitchen came the faint sound of the microwave beeping. Ian scrubbed his hand through his hair again. "What do you mean you didn't do any of that?"

"Come into the kitchen," I said. "We could both use a beer."

He followed me to the kitchen, sinking into a chair as I grabbed our beers and opened them. I handed one to him and he took a long swallow. I watched the way his throat worked, my cock twitching and letting me know that it was still very interested in taking Ian back to my bed.

I shoved the thought of a naked Ian on his hands and knees in my bed and sat down across from him. I took a swallow of beer and then set the beer bottle on the table. "Tell me exactly what you're talking about, Ian."

He sighed and picked at the label on the bottle. "Joe called me into his office right as I was leaving for the day. The teachers and the students know about Lori and Frank having sex in her classroom. Lori had whore spray-painted on her car and parents are calling Joe and demanding he fire Lori and Frank."

"Is Joe going to fire them?" I said.

"No. He has no proof that they were doing anything inappropriate. Anyway, Lori went to Joe and told him it was me who started the rumours because I'd seen them kissing in her classroom. Told him I was pissed off she had broken up with me. He pulled me into the office and reprimanded me for it, acted like I was some fucking little kid who was having a temper tantrum because the girl I liked didn't like me back. I told him I didn't say a word about Lori and Frank, and he had no proof that it was me. That maybe he should think twice about accusing someone of something without the fucking paperwork to back it up. I said…"

His voice died out and he stared at me. "Fuck me. I'm doing the exact same thing to you. I'm sorry."

I didn't say anything as Ian drank half his beer in two large gulps. He wiped his mouth with his hand and said, "I'm an asshole."

"You're not. But for the record, I didn't say anything to anyone about Lori and Frank. Why would you think I did?"

"Because you're pissed at me about Friday night," he said.

Confusion made my voice a little harsher than I intended. "Why would I be pissed at you?"

"Because I came so fast and then I didn't do anything for you, and then I avoided you all week," Ian said.

"Are you fucking kidding me?" I said. Ian's gaze landed on my mouth and fuck if that didn't make my cock get hard, even if I was gobsmacked by what he'd just said.

"What?" Ian said.

"Ian, I would never be angry just because a guy I was with climaxed quickly," I said. "I get that I come across as an asshole sometimes, but even I'm not that much of a dick."

He flushed and tore a strip from the beer label, rolling it between his fingers as he avoided my gaze. "I didn't do anything for you but before I could even offer, you were kicking me out of your house with a fake emergency text."

"It wasn't fake," I said. "My best friend Tristan really did text me and ask me to pick him up. I swear. I can show you the text messages if you'd like."

I sounded weird, and sort of desperate, but I hated the idea that Ian thought I was so ticked off because of his performance in the bedroom, I'd faked an emergency to get him out of my bed.

"No," he said. "I believe you. Sorry, I'm..." he blew his breath out. "Now I'm the one being an asshole, but I spent the entire week confused and angry and..."

"Full of regret about what we did," I said.

He glanced up at me, a frown crossing his face. "What? I don't regret it."

"I saw the look on your face, Ian, after we were finished," I said. "It was embarrassment and regret."

"Yeah, because I made such a fucking poor impression," Ian said. "I came in less than five minutes and then just laid there while you took care of yourself. I looked the way I did because I couldn't believe that happened. I'm not a guy who can go hours or anything, but I usually have some kind of stamina, and that night I just... didn't. It was shameful."

Relief washed over me, so deep that I felt almost giddy from it. "You don't regret what we did?"

"No," he stared steadily at me, "not at all. In fact, I spent most of my nights this week masturbating to the memory of it."

My cock pushed against the fabric of my pants. "You and me both."

His smile was two parts shy and two parts smug. "Oh yeah? Even with my poor performance?"

"Your performance was fine," I said.

He winced. "Fine isn't something to be proud of. Do you think..."

I raised an eyebrow at him. "Do I think what?"

"Do you think I could have another chance?"

I studied his mouth, smiling with satisfaction when redness creeped up his neck and he shifted in his chair. "You plan to give me an Oscar worthy performance. Is that right?"

"Well, maybe not Oscar worthy, but definitely Emmy. *Prime time* Emmy," he said.

I burst into laughter, and Ian chuckled as well before giving me a hopeful look. "What do you think?"

I stood and held out my hand. "Show me what you've got."

He took my hand and we walked to my bedroom. We were barely inside when Ian was tugging at my shirt. I lifted my arms and he yanked it over my head before dropping it on the floor. He pushed me up against the wall and kissed me hard. Fuck, I'd missed his taste. I kissed him back, his stubble scraping across my chin sent shivers down my spine.

He reached for my belt and unbuckled it. "Naked," he said against my mouth, "I want you naked."

"Ditto. Ditch the clothes," I said.

He grinned at me and we stripped off our clothes. I was already hard and aching and I stroked myself slowly as I watched Ian fumble to take off his socks. I studied his gorgeous cock, a bead of precum slipping out of my slit. I slicked my thumb across it and then held it in front of Ian's mouth. "Taste."

He immediately sucked on my thumb, his tongue cleaning away my cum.

"Delicious," he said.

I played with his nipples, giving them both a light pinch before I slid my hand up his chest and around to the back of his neck. I pushed lightly. "Why don't you have another taste."

"Yes, Will," he said as he sunk to his knees in front of me.

A shudder of need went down my back and more precum spilled from my dick. Ian leaned forward and licked it away. I moaned, my hips jerking forward and my hand tightening around the back of Ian's skull.

"Suck," I said.

Ian's lips closed around my dick and I was in heaven. I let my head fall back, closing my eyes and concentrating on the sensation of Ian's wet mouth, his warm tongue, the low sounds he made as he sucked. His method was a bit sloppy and a little timid, but it didn't fucking matter to me. I kept my hand on the back of his skull, holding him in place as I thrust rhythmically in and out of his mouth. I didn't go too deep, I didn't want to make him gag or feel uncomfortable, but to my surprise, Ian pushed forward enthusiastically, sucking down my dick to nearly the base.

"Fuuuuck," I moaned before staring down at him. "Baby, you're doing so fucking well."

He stared up at me with his mouth full of my cock, those

pretty blue eyes of his bringing up all sorts of emotions in me that were incredibly dangerous. I ran my fingers through his hair, tugging lightly on it as I continued to thrust. "Touch yourself, baby."

He reached down and jacked his dick with rough, hard strokes.

"Good," I said. "Play with my balls with your other hand."

He cupped my sac, his hand slowing down on his dick as he concentrated on teasing my balls with gentle strokes.

"Good," I moaned again. I jerked forward when Ian pressed against my taint, a harsh cry escaping my throat.

He pulled back, licking his red and swollen lips. "Sorry, did you, uh, not like that?"

I huffed out a laugh, my hand already pushing his mouth back to the head of my dick. "I liked it. Keep sucking."

He took me into his mouth again. He was focusing on his own dick again, his free hand now clutching at my thigh, but I was all for it. Watching Ian touch himself while he had my dick in his mouth was a fucking fantasy come true.

He was sucking hard and fast, my cock sliding back and forth between his lips like it was meant to be there. I groaned, my entire body shuddering as I grew closer to my climax. I wanted desperately to cum in Ian's mouth, wanted to watch him swallow all of it, but I couldn't ask him for that. He wouldn't be comfortable with that.

"I'm gonna cum," I told him. "Finish me off with your hand."

He made a sound of disapproval in the back of his throat and sucked me harder and deeper. I cried out, my hips bucking forward. "Ian! Baby, I can't hold back... I can't..."

His hands clutched at my ass, squeezing tightly and holding me in place as he sucked. With a harsh cry, my back arched, and I shot my load down Ian's throat. He swallowed rapidly, his gaze never leaving mine as I twitched and shook and moaned his name.

I was still cupping his skull and I made myself release him before the poor guy passed out from lack of oxygen. Ian pulled back and sucked in a breath, then licked the last of my cum from his bottom lip.

I hauled him to his feet and pushed him back against the wall. I angled my mouth over his as I reached for his cock. He cried out into my mouth when I wrapped my fingers around his shaft and pumped him firmly.

I could taste myself on his tongue and it sent fresh desire through my body. We kissed hard and rough, our tongues battling for control as Ian's body tensed. His hands dug into my arms and he made a harsh cry into my mouth as he orgasmed. Hot, sticky cum spilled over both of our stomachs. I stroked him until the last of his cum spurted out and he started to soften in my hand.

He was shuddering and moaning, and I rested my forehead on his, his cum gluing our flat abdomens together as we both came down from our orgasm high.

"Holy fuck," Ian panted. "That was…"

"Amazing," I said.

"Yeah," he said.

I pressed a kiss against his mouth, smiling at him when he said, "So, uh, how was I at, um…"

My grin widened. "Baby, your cock sucking skills are definitely Oscar worthy."

He laughed and kissed my throat. "I'm all sticky now."

"Me too. Have you eaten dinner?"

He shook his head. "No, I came over here straight from the school."

"I was heating up some leftovers. Why don't we have a quick shower, and then you can stay for dinner," I said.

He stared at me. "You sure? I can leave. I know this isn't -"

"I want you to stay," I said.

He grinned boyishly. "Cool."

CHAPTER 9

IAN

"Thanks for dinner," I said as I loaded mine and Will's dishes into the dishwasher. "You're a really great cook."

Will shrugged as he wiped off the island with a cloth. "It was just leftovers."

"Delicious leftovers." I closed the dishwasher. "I'm not a great cook, but I'm really great at cleaning up afterward."

Will laughed and hung the cloth over the side of the sink. "Well, I'll gladly cook you dinner anytime if it means I don't have to clean up the mess."

I leaned against the island as an awkward silence descended. I should probably leave Will's place, even though I had a couple of hours until I met Rachel and Tabitha at Sapphire's.

Do you even want to go to Sapphire's now?

No, not really. But I had told Rachel and Tabitha I would, and I wouldn't bail on them. Not when they were doing this for me. Besides, I didn't know for sure that Will wanted to keep doing this, despite what had happened earlier.

So, ask him, idiot. Then you'll know.

My inner voice made a good point. I didn't even know why I was so nervous. Will and I seemed compatible and I'd actually done something for him this time instead of making him do all the work.

I cleared my throat. "So, uh -"

"You want to watch some Netflix?" Will said. "I've been thinking about starting a re-watch of *Justified*."

"I've never seen that show," I said.

The horror on Will's face was almost comical. "You've never seen *Justified*?"

"No, it's, like, a western or something, right?"

Will shook his head before grabbing my hand and leading me out of the kitchen. "A western or something... good God, man. I can't believe you've gone this long without watching a single episode of Timothy Olyphant in a cowboy hat and tight jeans..."

I laughed and sank onto the couch beside him as he turned on the television and switched to the Netflix app. He searched for the show, hit play, and tossed his phone on the coffee table in front of us. His thigh was warm against mine and I had a really weird urge to put my arm around him and cuddle him. I resisted. We weren't dating and I'd look like a fucking loser if I tried to make this into something more than it was.

"WELL?" WILL'S VOICE WAS EXCITED LIKE A LITTLE KID hopped up on too much cotton candy. "What do you think?"

"It's pretty good," I said.

"Pretty good?" Now he looked like I'd crushed every last

one of his dreams. "*Pretty good?*" He took a deep breath and pinched the bridge of his nose. "Okay, Will, don't panic. He's only seen a couple of episodes."

I laughed and poked him in the thigh. "Do you need to do some deep breathing exercises, or maybe some yoga to help combat the stress of your disappointment?"

"It's fine," he said. "You just need to watch a few more episodes, then you'll be hooked as I am."

He went to start the next episode and I said, "Oh, uh, actually, I need to get going."

He tensed before nodding. "Okay."

"I have plans with Rachel and Tabitha," I said.

"Right." His face carefully composed, he shut off the television.

"We're going to Sapphire's," I said.

His nostrils flared, and he turned to face me before gripping the back of my head and pulling me forward. He gave me a searing kiss, one that turned my insides to jelly and my cock to a stiff spike.

"Go to that fucking meat market tonight," he growled against my lips. "but just remember that it's me who gets to fuck your gorgeous, tight ass for the first time. Don't even think about going home with someone, Ian."

Hot pleasure at his possessiveness washed over me. I swallowed hard. "So, you want to continue with this?"

He leaned back, his hand still gripping the back of my neck. "I do. Why would you think I wouldn't?"

"I wasn't sure because of how I bulldozed my way in here accusing you of... anyway, I wouldn't blame you if you didn't want to keep showing me some, um, stuff."

He grinned at me. "I definitely want to keep showing you some, um, stuff, Ian."

I laughed and pressed a kiss against his mouth. "Good. Come to Sapphire's with me?"

"Sure," he said.

"Really?" I stared at him in surprise.

He laughed. "Yes. If you hadn't invited me, I would have shown up anyway like some weirdo stalker."

"Honey, with a dick like yours, you can stalk me anytime," I said.

Will laughed again before nipping at my neck. "C'mon, let's get out of here. The sooner we get to Sapphire's, the sooner we can make an excuse to leave so I can bring you back here and get you naked again."

I made a breathless moan when he sucked on my earlobe. "I like that idea."

WILL

"So," RACHEL EYED ME OVER HER DRINK LIKE SHE WAS A hawk and I was a field mouse, "what exactly is your game with Ian?"

I glanced at the dance floor where Ian was dancing with Tabitha and a bunch of random women they'd made friends with. I wasn't surprised by Rachel's question, and I wasn't offended either. If it were Tristan, I'd be acting the same way as Rachel.

"No game," I said.

"Oh yeah? Because it doesn't look that way from where I'm sitting," Rachel said.

"I know, but I promise you I'm not. There was some miscommunication between us, but we've cleared it up."

"Meaning you're going to be both his break-up rebound

and help him clear up any confusion he has regarding his sexuality."

I tried not to wince at her words. It wasn't like I didn't know that I was just a rebound and experiment for Ian, but, fuck, if it didn't wound me to hear it said out loud.

"That's right," I said.

"This will sound cliché as fuck, but if you hurt him, I'll hurt you," Rachel said.

It was me who'd wind up hurt. I was already way too possessive of Ian and acting like we were dating, but I smiled and said, "I know, and I won't hurt him."

Ian and Tabitha joined us, both of them sweaty and flushed from dancing. Ian took one look at me and said, "What's wrong?"

"Nothing." I made my smile large. "You looked like you were having fun."

Ian studied Rachel. "What did you say to him, Rach?"

"Nothing," she said. "Relax, Ian."

Tabitha flung a friendly arm around my shoulders. "Did she give her 'you hurt him, I hurt you' speech?"

I laughed. "Maybe."

"She's famous for it," Tabitha said. "She says it to all our new boyfriends. So, welcome to the club, my friend."

"Oh, um, he's not my boyfriend," Ian said quickly. "We're just…"

"Having fun," I supplied as my stomach twisted and turned and tumbled.

"Nothing wrong with some fun," Tabitha said. "Speaking of which, let's get back out on the dance floor. Will, you interested in joining us?"

I glanced at my watch. "Actually, I think I'll head home. It's late."

"It's barely one o'clock," Tabitha said. "You've only had one drink and you haven't danced at all."

"I'm not much of a dancer," I said, "and I have an early workout tomorrow."

"Who works out on a Saturday morning?" Tabitha said, but she pecked me on the cheek before taking Ian and Rachel's hand. "C'mon, you two, let's do this."

"I'm going to go too," Ian said.

I tried not to let my relief show. I didn't want to leave Ian here alone, but I'd never been much for the bar scene and I was at my limit.

Or are you just pouting because Ian made it perfectly clear you're nothing but a good time to him?

I ignored my inner voice as Ian kissed Rachel and Tabitha before standing next to me. "Ready to go?"

I nodded. "Nice to see you, ladies. Enjoy the rest of your night."

IAN CLIMBED OUT OF THE UBER AND CLEARED HIS THROAT, staring at his car in my driveway. The Uber pulled away and we stood silently for a few minutes before I said, "I had fun, thanks for inviting me."

"Did you?" he said. "It kind of seemed like you were just counting the minutes until you could leave."

"I'm not much of a partier," I said, "and I usually prefer a pub over a bar."

"Then why did you go with me?" Ian said.

I should have lied, but my head – or maybe it was my heart – wouldn't let me. "I wanted to spend more time with you."

A smile crossed Ian's face. He stepped closer and took my

hand, banishing both the space and the awkwardness between us. "Oh yeah?"

"Yeah," I said.

His thumb brushed across my knuckles. "I'm glad you did. I like spending time with you too."

This is just a rebound and experiment for him, I reminded myself. *Nothing more.*

Still, it didn't stop me from stepping closer and pressing a brief kiss against his mouth. "How much did you drink tonight?"

"Couple of beers," he said. "A shot earlier in the night with Rachel."

I glanced at his car. "You probably shouldn't drive, just to be on the safe side."

"Probably not," he said, "just to be on the safe side."

"Then it's settled." I led him to the house, opening the door and stepping inside. "You can sleep in my guest room tonight."

He stared at me and I laughed before pulling him into the house and shutting the door behind him. "I'm kidding, Ian."

"Oh, you're gonna get it for that," Ian said.

"Get it?" I arched an eyebrow. "What exactly am I going to get? Be specific."

Ian's laugh turned into a low moan when I pushed him up against the wall and devoured his mouth. I took my time tasting him, wanting to drive him as crazy with need as he did me. I pressed against him, our hard cocks lining up perfectly against each other. Ian rubbed against me, the friction making me wild.

"My bedroom, now," I said.

"I'm sweaty from dancing," he said. "You mind if I take a shower first?"

I shook my head. "You mind if I join you?"

His grin was slow and delicious. "I was hoping you'd ask."

CHAPTER 10

IAN

The water sluicing down Will's perfect ass, made it impossible for me to keep my hands off my cock. I pumped my dick with slow strokes and watched as Will ducked his dark head under the shower and let the water wash away the soap that still clung to his body.

When he turned and saw me with my dick in my hand, he gave me a look of disapproval that only made me hotter. "No touching yourself, Ian."

"I had to do something while you hogged all the hot water," I said.

He laughed and kissed me while he slid his wet body past mine. His shower was small, but, honestly, I didn't mind. The more excuses I had to touch Will, the better. He cupped my ass, giving it a squeeze before pushing me under the spray of the shower.

"Need some help washing your back?"

"Yes, please," I said.

I soaped the front of my body quickly, hissing in pleasure

when I cleaned my aching dick. Fuck, I really wanted Will's mouth on my dick again. I handed the soap to Will and moaned happily when his strong hands kneaded my shoulders and then stroked across my upper back.

"Fuck, that feels good," I said.

I reached to stroke my dick again, but Will knocked my hand away. "No cumming, Ian. Not yet."

I grumbled under my breath, but Will's hands on my ass was a sudden and welcome distraction. He kneaded my ass cheeks before his slippery soapy fingers delved into the crack. I tensed when he ran his fingers over my hole. I didn't want to tense, but it was an involuntary action. Will leaned forward, his fingers rubbing lightly over my hole and kissed a soap-free spot on my shoulder.

"Relax, baby. Just cleaning for now, nothing more."

I relaxed at his words, although the 'for now' part of his sentence had me immediately all up in my head about what might happen once we got out of the shower. Will hadn't seemed in a particular hurry to fuck my ass, but he could have changed his mind, right?

"Tell me what you're thinking." Will's mouth moved to my neck and he nipped lightly.

I took a shuddering breath, my cock dripping precum and my thoughts scattered. "Uh, just about what we might do later."

He kissed my throat again. "I told you before that fucking your ass isn't the end all, be all."

"I know," I said. "But I want you to know that I'm ready for it, if you want to do it."

Was I? I didn't know for sure. But I did know that it was incredibly important to me that I please Will in bed. Important that I made him want me and only me for the rest of his –

I cut that thought off hard and fast. Despite our connection, despite how good the sex was between us, I wasn't in the proper headspace for a relationship right now. I was still reeling from my break-up with Lori and learning to trust someone again would take time.

You trust Will.

Will stopped touching me and I ducked my head under the water, letting the soap rinse away. Trusting Will wasn't a mistake exactly, more like... naïve thinking. I barely knew the guy. Besides, even though I believed that he wouldn't cheat on me or lie to me like Lori had, I wasn't getting seriously involved with a co-worker ever again. It was a terrible idea. I'd almost gotten fired today because of it.

"Ian?" Will's arms slid around my waist, his hands warm on my stomach. "You okay?"

"Yeah," I said. I shut the water off and we stepped out of the shower, both of us toweling dry. It was awkward between us, and that was my fault.

"If you've changed your mind and want to go home -"

"I haven't," I said quickly.

"You sure?" Will stood naked in the small bathroom, the towel bunched in his hand, his erection down to a semi now, thanks to me and my stupidity.

I mentally shook off any stronger and confusing feelings for Will that might be developing. I could examine them more deeply when I was by myself and make a damn list if I had to of why it was a mistake. I smiled at him. "Positive."

I took the towel from him and hung it up neatly beside mine before taking his hand. We walked into his bedroom and Will pressed a kiss against my mouth. "Lie on your stomach on the bed."

My already knotted nerves tightened further when Will took lube out of the nightstand drawer. Hoping he didn't see my nerves on my face, I laid down on the bed on my stomach. I told myself to relax as Will straddled my hips.

To my surprise, his hands kneaded my shoulders and then my upper back. He leaned over and pressed a kiss between my shoulder blades. "Take some deep breaths, Ian."

I breathed deep, the tension and anxiety melting away as Will worked the big muscles in my back. He pressed a path up and down my spine and I groaned happily, my back arching when he found a knot in my upper back and kneaded it out.

"Fuck, that feels so good," I mumbled into the pillow.

"Good." Will shifted lower, straddling my thighs now as he worked his strong hands over my lower back.

"Oh God, yeah, right there," I grunted with pleasure.

By the time Will started to rub my ass, any anxiety I felt was completely gone. I was a pile of blissful goo on the bed and the only emotion I registered was how good Will's touch felt. When he bent and kissed the top of my ass, I made a low moan of pleasure. He kissed and nipped at my ass cheeks. My cock was stirring to life again and I rubbed against the quilt, moaning quietly when Will squeezed my ass again.

He pulled my cheeks apart and I waited for the touch of his fingers against me. I wasn't anxious, Will's massage had made it nearly impossible to be nervous anymore, but I was a little surprised that I hadn't heard him reaching for the lube. I knew that spit was an option, but why use spit when lube was right – holy fuck!

I reared up at the first touch of Will's tongue against my hole. If Will hadn't been holding my ass cheeks open, they would have clenched shut at the unexpected sensation. As it was, my hands grabbed large fistfuls of sheet and I cried out as Will licked me again.

"Will!" My voice was strangled. "Wh-what are you doing?"

He didn't reply, his tongue too busy licking me in a spot that I shouldn't have found so pleasurable but did.

"Oh, oh God," I moaned. "Will, I can't... oh fuck..."

My whole body shuddered when Will licked around that tight ring of muscle. I had no idea how sensitive it would be, or how much pleasure I would feel from the warm wetness of Will's tongue.

When he stiffened his tongue and pressed it against my hole, I couldn't stop my loud cry of pleasure or the way my feet drummed on the bed. My cock was leaking so much precum, the sheet was a wet and sticky mess underneath me.

I gasped and moaned and made inarticulate begging noises. Will gave me one final lick before sliding off of me and lying on his side next to me. "Face me, baby."

My heart knocking against my ribs, my cock so hard it hurt, I turned to face Will as he grabbed the bottle of lube from the nightstand. His cock pressed against my stomach and he moaned quietly when I stroked his dick.

He slid his arm around my waist. When his fingers pressed between my ass cheeks, they were slippery and cool with lube. I gasped and Will kissed the back of my shoulder. "It's okay, baby. Just my fingers, all right?"

"Yeah, okay," I moaned.

The tip of Will's finger pressed against my hole. I tensed and Will kissed my shoulder with open mouth and wet tongue. "No, baby. Relax. It's going to feel so good, I promise."

I moaned and relaxed, gasping again when Will's finger slipped past my tight ring of muscle up to the first knuckle. "Okay?"

I stared into his dark eyes. "Yeah, good."

He smiled and we kissed hotly, our tongues touching and tasting each other as Will slid his finger in and out of my ass.

He released my mouth and smiled again at me. "How does that feel? Any pain?"

"No," I said. "No pain, but it doesn't feel... uh, pleasurable."

He kissed my throat, the rough stubble on his face sent goosebumps rising to life along my spine. He added another finger and stretched me a little. There was an increased feeling of fullness but still no pain. I was happy about that. I wanted to take Will's cock and all early signs indicated that I might be able to do it with less pain than I thought. Not that two fingers were comparable to Will's thick cock, but still... it gave me hope.

"Okay?" Will asked, as he scissored his fingers gently.

"Yes," I said. "Still good. No pain but no, um, pleasure either." I hated to admit that, but I couldn't lie to Will about this.

"Not yet, huh?" He pushed his fingers in a little deeper.

"No," I said, "but I'd be still willing to fu...uuuck!"

Will's low chuckle was lost in my almost feral howl of pleasure. He'd brushed against a spot, a spot that made my body twitch, my knees weak, and my cock stiff. He pressed it again and I groaned his name before reaching down and wrapping my hand around my dick.

I rubbed furiously, gasping for breath as Will rubbed and pressed that magic spot. I came and came fucking hard less than thirty seconds later. Cum covered the sheets and my abdomen as I made a long drawn out cry of pleasure and jerked mercilessly at my dick.

I was only vaguely aware of Will withdrawing his hand. He rolled me over to my other side and crowded close, his dick wedged in the crack of my ass, and his arm around me and holding my shaking body tight against. His hips pumped furiously, his dick sliding up and down the crack of my ass as his warm breath washed over my heated skin. I moaned happily when I felt the first spurts of his cum coat my lower back.

He bit me in the tender spot where my neck met my shoulder, groaning quietly as he came all over my back. When he was finished, he collapsed on his back, one hand rubbing my hip as we both fought to catch our breaths.

I was covered in my cum and Will's cum and I couldn't have been fucking happier. My body still shaking, I made a mumbled, "hmm?" when Will said my name.

"You okay?" he said.

"Uh-huh." I craned my neck to stare at him over my shoulder. "Hey, Will?"

"Yeah?"

"I think I'm into ass play."

His grin turned into a full-out belly laugh when I said, "But just to be sure, we should probably try that a couple more times."

"Deal," he said before kissing the back of my shoulder. "But it's late, so what do you say we have another quick shower, change the sheets, and get some rest. We can test your newfound love for ass play again in the morning."

"You want me to stay the night?"

Will bit at his bottom lip before studying a spot on the wall over my shoulder. "I'd like you to, but don't feel obligated to stay."

"I want to," I said quickly.

"Good." Will's face relaxed and he rubbed my hip. "Come on. Let's get you cleaned up."

IAN

STANDING IN WILL'S KITCHEN, WEARING A PAIR OF HIS shorts and cooking him breakfast felt way righter than it should have. I hummed quietly to myself as I finished the eggs and slid them onto a plate. I couldn't cook worth shit, but I knew how to fry an egg and put some bread in the toaster.

Will was sleeping soundly when I'd woken. A little surprising, considering it was almost ten and he was a self-professed early riser. Of course, it had been closer to three before we'd fallen asleep.

I buttered the toast and added it to the plate. Making breakfast for Will felt damn good. Like, 'I could do this every morning for the rest of my life' good.

Whoa, bud. Slow down. Will made it perfectly clear that he's not interested in a relationship with you, just like you made that point perfectly clear to him. Don't let your little crush on him feel like something more just because the man knows how to tickle your prostate.

My inner voice made excellent points. Ones I would have to acknowledge and pay attention to... but not this morning. No, this morning was for breakfast in bed with a really hot guy, and then maybe a few hours of slow exploration of all the new things I might like. Hell, maybe Will would even fuck me. It wasn't completely out of the realm of possibilities, right?

I belted out the chorus of my favourite Conway Twitty song, not even a little ashamed that I was singing loud enough to wake Will up and he would realize I was a fan of classic country. I knew it wasn't cool to love country music, Lori had drilled that into me the last two years, but I suddenly didn't give a fuck. Will wasn't the kind to judge me for my music tastes.

I heard Will's footsteps as he walked into the kitchen. I sang the last of the chorus again, wiggling my ass at him before picking up the two plates of eggs and toast. "You were supposed to let me wake you up with breakfast in bed followed by a make your toes curl dick sucking from yours truly, but since you're up now," I turned to face him, "maybe we should…"

My throat went dry and I almost dropped the plates of food. I stared in a combination of shock and growing horror at the middle-aged couple, who were most definitely not Will, standing in the kitchen.

"I, uh… are you, sorry, am I…"

The man, he was tall and lean and the spitting image of Will only with silver hair and blue eyes, arched an eyebrow at me. "Are you a friend of my son's?"

"I'd say he's more than a friend," the woman said with a grin. She had blonde hair cut into a stylish bob and the same dark eyes as Will.

Will's father's face went slack, and his eyes widened. "Are you… oh my God, is our son gay?"

My shock disappeared to be swallowed fully by horror. Oh, holy fuck, I had just fucking outed Will to his own parents.

"Oh, uh, I'm, I mean Will and I work, I mean, we're not…" I couldn't think, couldn't speak. Will was going to fucking kill me.

"Oh, Ronald." The woman smacked Will's father on the chest. "Stop torturing the poor boy." She smiled at me. "We know Will is gay, honey."

I went weak with relief. My hands were shaking from the

dump of adrenaline and I set the plates on the counter before I dropped them on the floor.

Will's dad was laughing loudly, literally holding his belly as the laughter spilled out of him. "Oh God, the look on your face, kid… shit, I should have taken a picture."

"Ronnie, you're terrible," Will's mother said. She held her hand out and I shook it numbly. "I'm Margaret, and this is Ronald. We're Will's parents. And you are?"

"Uh, I'm Ian," I said as I shook Ronald's hand.

"It's lovely to meet you, Ian," Margaret said.

I suddenly felt terribly exposed in just a pair of Will's shorts. I crossed my arms over my chest and cleared my throat. "I'm sorry, I didn't hear you come in."

"Well, you were singing quite loudly," Margaret said. "You have a lovely voice."

"Um, thank you."

"Is Will still in bed?" Ronald said. "It's not like him to sleep in this late. In fact -"

"You know," Will strolled into the kitchen wearing a pair of sleep pants and a t-shirt, "the key I gave you is for emergencies only."

He kissed his mother's cheek and fist-bumped his dad. "Why are you here so early?"

"Early?" Ronald said. "It's ten-thirty on a Saturday. Also, you were supposed to meet us at the farmer's market at nine."

"Shit," Will said. "I forgot."

"Obviously," Margaret said with another small smile aimed at me. "But it's open until one, so get dressed. Also, why haven't you introduced us to your new boyfriend?"

"Ian's not my boyfriend," Will said so quickly that I winced a little. "We're work colleagues."

"Work colleagues," Margaret said, the skepticism in her voice laid on thick.

Will flushed but nodded. "Yes. He teaches athletics."

"That must be why you're in such good shape," Margaret said to me. I blushed brightly and she grinned before saying, "Would you like to join us at the market, Ian? It's -"

"He can't," Will said. "He has other plans this morning and was just leaving. Right, Ian?"

"Yes," I said.

Ignoring the embarrassment and the weird amount of hurt coursing through my body, I said, "It, uh, it was nice to meet you, Mr. and Mrs. Matthews." and left the kitchen. I dressed in record time and grabbed my phone, masking my disappointment when Will didn't join me in his bedroom.

I lingered at the front door, putting my shoes on more slowly than I needed to, but when Will didn't make an appearance, I gave up and left, hurrying to my car and feeling like I'd royally screwed up.

CHAPTER 11

WILL

I stood next to my car in the parking lot of Ian's condo building, one hand on the door handle and the other one holding my phone. This was probably a bad idea, right? Like, a terrible fucking idea. At the very least, I should text him before I knocked on his door. Who showed up to their casual sex partner's place for a booty call without texting first?

Casual sex partner? He's more than that and you know it. You've spent the entire day wishing you could be with him. Hell, even your dad could tell you were distracted, and he never notices anything.

I stared at my phone, indecision still keeping me beside my car. I'd panicked a little this morning when my parents showed up. Not only had I forgotten my plans with them, which was unlike me, but hearing my mom refer to Ian as my boyfriend had sent a longing through me that I hadn't felt in a long time.

It was stupid to want a relationship with Ian, so why did I spend the entire time at the farmer's market, envisioning what it would be like to have Ian with me? His hand in mine, his low laugh and gorgeous smile lighting up the whole fucking place.

I sighed and unlocked my car. Ian didn't want anything serious, and there was no guarantee that even if my parents hadn't shown up, that he wouldn't have taken off after breakfast anyway.

Before I could climb into my car, my phone chimed in my hand. My mouth went dry and I stared at the message.

Ian: *You gonna stand in my parking lot all night or come up?*

My heart thudding, I walked to the front door of the building. My phone chimed again and I read Ian's message.

Ian: *Seventh floor, apartment twelve.*

The front door buzzed. I opened it and stepped into the foyer. On the seventh floor, I went left and followed the numbered doors to twelve. I raised my hand to knock but Ian opened the door first.

"Hey, come on in."

I stepped inside, toeing off my shoes and giving my jacket to Ian so he could hang it in the front closet.

"So, I guess you have a view of the parking lot, huh?" I said, as I followed him down the hall and into the living area. It was open concept with the kitchen and the living room separated by a butcher block topped island. It was on the smaller side but perfect for Ian.

And until recently Lori as well. Don't forget about that.

I wouldn't.

"Yeah," he said with a small grin. "I was gaming and the window next to the couch overlooks the lot."

"Sorry I didn't call first."

"No problem. You want a beer? Juice? Water?"

"Water would be good."

Ian got us both waters and I followed him to the couch. We sank down on it and I stared at the paused screen of Ian's video game. "Sorry, I interrupted your game."

He just shrugged and took a swig of water. "Did you have fun with your parents?"

"About that..." I took a deep breath. "I shouldn't have hurried you out of there so quickly. It was a dick thing to do."

To my surprise, Ian said, "Nah, it wasn't."

"I saw the look on your face," I said. "I hurt your feelings and -"

"Yeah, at first," he said, "but that's on me, not you. We've both been perfectly clear what this is with each other, and me hanging out with you and your parents doesn't fall within the," he hesitated, "parameters of what this is."

"The parameters," I said.

He nodded before grinning at me. "It's all good, Will."

"You're not pissed at me for telling my parents you were just a work colleague?"

"No. We are just work colleagues," Ian said with a nonchalance that made my guts twist. "Maybe we're a little more right now, but once we have sex, we'll go back to being work colleagues and friends, right? Hell, after last night and how much I enjoyed what we did, it's possible we'll be back to work colleagues by Monday."

His flirty grin, normally something that would have made me ache to kiss him, sent nausea rolling through me. Ian expected we would have sex tonight. And when that happened, what was happening between us was over. Just like that.

My urge to get angry, to lash out at him over finding it so easy to end whatever this was between us, was overwhelming. I made myself take a deep breath. Ian wasn't saying or doing anything wrong. This was the agreement between us and just because I wanted more, didn't give me the right to be angry that he didn't. I just had to accept that this was the last weekend I'd ever see Ian naked again.

Or you could put off having sex with him for a little longer.

"Will? You okay?" Ian said. "Look, if I made an assumption about why you've come over, I apologize. We don't have to do anything if -"

"No," I said, "it's what I'm here for."

"Good." Ian put his hand on my thigh and rubbed lightly. Despite my inner turmoil, my cock started to harden. Fuck, did I want this man.

If you take him tonight, you'll never have these moments with him again.

Ian's hand was sliding toward my crotch, and I pushed it away in almost a panic. Ian stared at me in puzzlement. "What's wrong?"

"Nothing," I said, "I'm, uh... hungry."

Ian laughed. "I guess it is close to dinner. You want to order in a pizza?"

"Yes," I said.

"Cool." He was pulling up the app on his phone and I reached out and took his hand.

"Hey, I want to be with you, but I think we shouldn't have sex tonight."

He frowned at me. "Why not?"

"I think it's smarter to give it a little longer, make sure that you're fully on board with the idea."

My back sweating, I waited for Ian to tell me I was being ridiculous. Hell, even to me the words coming out of my mouth was some weak ass shit. To my surprise, Ian nodded and said, "Yeah, okay. That makes sense. At least for tonight."

A little giddy with relief, I pointed at the television screen, "Order the pizza and then I'll kick your ass at GTA."

Ian laughed. "Deal."

I SAT ON THE SIDE OF IAN'S BED AND STUDIED HIM IN THE early morning light peeking through the half-open blinds. He was lying on his stomach, his arms tucked under his pillow and the sheet barely covering his gorgeous ass.

My mouth went dry as I traced a finger down his spine to the top of his ass. Last night, we'd done everything but fucking. Despite how many times I'd cum last night, my cock pressed against my jeans as I stared at Ian's ass. Fuck, the desire to just strip off my clothes, climb back into Ian's bed and give him what he wanted – what we *both* wanted – was almost too difficult to resist.

I palmed Ian's ass, stroking lightly as he sighed softly and shifted on the bed. I didn't have to leave. I wasn't meeting Tristan until later today. But if I didn't leave, I would fuck Ian. I knew that as well as I knew my own name.

If you fuck him, it's over.

My inner voice was right. If I gave in to my urge, I'd leave Ian's bed later this morning and never return to it. We'd be work colleagues only. My stomach flipped and flopped. We wouldn't even be friends. I couldn't be friends with Ian, couldn't hang out with him outside of work when I wouldn't be allowed to touch him or kiss him.

I swallowed hard and rubbed at my forehead. I could put off seeing Ian this week, claim that I was busy with work or family commitments, and maybe – maybe – put off fucking him on Friday night with another lame-ass excuse about needing to be sure he wanted this. But the odds were that by this time next week, my cock would be deep in Ian's perfect ass.

The thought filled me with a weird combination of deep-seated longing and dread that did nothing to help my nausea. I needed to leave before I fucked Ian and then did something incredibly stupid like beg him for a relationship.

I leaned over Ian and kissed him on the cheek, squeezing his hip until his eyelids fluttered open. He stared blearily at me. "Will? Wha' time?"

Shit, he was adorable. I might have been an early riser, but Ian most definitely was not.

"Early," I said. "I gotta go. I'm meeting a friend for a workout at the gym, and then having lunch with Tristan."

"Sure, okay," Ian said before yawning. His eyes drifted shut. "Call me later?"

He was snoring quietly before I could even reply. I hesitated and kissed his cheek again before burying my face in the side of his neck for a few seconds. I stood and headed to the door of his bedroom, pausing in the doorway to study him for a moment.

What this man did to me. And he had no fucking idea.

CHAPTER 12

WILL

"You shouldn't fuck him." Tristan stretched his long legs out in front of him. After we ate lunch, he'd returned to my place to watch a movie.

"That's what I've been saying," I said. "But I don't know how much longer I can keep putting him off about it."

"No," Tristan pointed his half-eaten apple at me. "What I mean is you shouldn't fuck him at all."

I scowled at him before collapsing on the couch next to him. "Why not?"

"Because you like him." Tristan bit into his apple.

"Of course I like him," I said. "I wouldn't fuck him if I didn't."

Tristan chewed and swallowed. "Don't be deliberately obtuse. You like Ian a fuck of a lot more than you should, especially since you know for a fact that he is neither ready nor wants to be in a relationship again."

"Don't sugar coat it or anything," I said.

His look was sympathetic. "You know I'm right. Sleeping

with him would be a mistake. I know you, Will. You won't be able to walk away after that. It's not who you are."

"What's that supposed to mean?" I said.

"It means that you give off this tough, nothing ever fucks me up vibe, when you're actually sensitive and," he paused in thought, "tender-hearted."

"Tender-hearted? Okay, *Mom*," I said with a grimace. "Since when does a guy your fucking age use words like sensitive and tender-hearted?"

Tristan laughed. "Whatever, shithead. You know I'm right. The point I'm trying to make is that you're in love with Ian and you're gonna get your heart broken again if you don't walk away now."

"I'm not in love with him. I barely know him," I said.

Tristan shrugged. "So what? You can fall in love with someone you barely know. Happens all the time."

"Name one person outside of the fucking movies," I said.

"You. You fall hard and fast for a guy, Will, you always have. In university, it was James and then that guy, fuck, what was his name… it was a cow thing… uh, Holstein or…"

"Angus, you dick. His name was Angus," I said with a grudging laugh.

"Right. Angus. You guys were talking marriage and kids within six months of meeting each other. And most recently, it was Mike. You were in love with him by the end of your second date."

I wanted to keep arguing, but Tristan was right. I did tend to fall hard and fast. Still, these feelings I had for Ian felt different to me. Stronger. More… *there* in a tangible way that I had a hard time understanding.

I shook my head. What I was feeling was just because I'd never waited so long to fuck someone before. My lust for him was mixing with my affection and making everything seem more intense. That was the simplest explanation.

But not necessarily the correct one.

"You shouldn't sleep with him," Tristan repeated.

"Yeah, I know," I said. "I'll end it with him before I fuck him."

"Good." Tristan glanced at his watch. "Shit, I gotta go."

"It's almost dinner," I said. "I'm making chicken cacciatore if you want to stay."

"Thanks, but I can't." Tristan headed to the kitchen to toss his apple core into the garbage. "I told Lance I'd meet him over at O'Keefe's for dinner."

"Since when did you become such a social butterfly?" I said as I followed him.

He shrugged. "If I'm sitting at home, I'm thinking about Shepherd and how much I want him to fuck me. Like, to an obsessively unhealthy amount. So, I do things… cheap things thanks to my current lack of money. But I figure I spend enough time during the week wondering what it would be like to be under him. I don't need to spend my weekends doing the same thing."

Shit, I'd been so wrapped up in my own issues with Ian, that I hadn't given a thought to Tristan and his boss problems. "Maybe you should look for another shop to work at," I said. "I mean, if Shepherd hates you as much as you say he does, doesn't it stand to reason that you might get fired?"

"Probably not. Like I said before, he actually lets me work on the classic cars, and there's never been anyone else in the shop but him who's allowed to even breathe on them." Ian grabbed his jacket from the closet next to the front door.

"Okay," I said, "but still, it can't be fun to work with a guy you're that attracted to but will never fuck."

Tristan grinned at me. "It isn't. And you're about to find out just how much it sucks."

"Shit," I said.

Tristan clapped me on the back before opening the door. "Tough luck, my -"

We both stared in surprise at Ian who was standing on my front porch with his hand raised to knock. "Hi," he said after a few seconds of silence.

"Hey," I said.

Ian was studying Tristan and was that jealousy in his eyes or just my wishful thinking?

"Ian, this is Tristan. Tristan, this is a work colleague Ian."

"Nice to meet you." Tristan held out his hand and Ian shook it.

I knew for certain I wasn't imagining the relief in Ian's face or voice when he said, "It's good to meet you too."

Ian glanced at me. "Sorry, I should have texted first. I assumed that you'd be free by now."

He started to back down the porch steps. "I'll see you tomorrow at work."

"I was just leaving," Tristan said. "You should stay. You and Will have a lot to talk about."

I cheerfully pictured throttling Tristan with my bare hands as Ian stared uncertainly at me. "Do we?"

"Come in, Ian. Tristan, I'll text you later." I gave Tristan a look that said, *I'm going to fucking kill you the next time I see you.*

Tristan grinned at me, the jackass knew exactly what I was thinking, before clapping me on the back. "See you later, Will."

I closed the door behind Ian. "Sorry I left so early this morning."

"That's fine. Do you want to have dinner with me? My treat," Ian said.

"You bought dinner yesterday," I said.

"It was just pizza," Ian said with a laugh.

I hesitated. A very big part of me wanted to go for dinner, wanted to pretend it was a date and that Ian wanted more from me than he actually did. Before I could succumb to the madness of saying yes, I said, "I have dinner plans."

"Oh. Right, of course. It was stupid of me to just drop by without calling." Ian's face was flushed, and I hated how awkward and uncomfortable I'd made him feel. "I'll see you tomorrow at work."

Knowing I was being stupid but hating the idea of sending him away, I grabbed his arm when he reached for the door. "I meant I have plans for making dinner. Why don't you stay and join me? Do you like chicken cacciatore?"

"I do," Ian said slowly, "but I don't want to intrude."

"You're not," I said.

"Are you sure? I get it if you want some time alone," he said. "I won't be offended or anything. Lori needed a lot of alone time."

"I'm not your ex-girlfriend," I said. My voice was harsh, and Ian recoiled slightly.

"I know, I didn't mean… shit, that was a dumb thing to say."

I sighed, rubbing at my forehead where a dull throb had started. "Sorry. I have a headache and I'm tired."

"I'll go," Ian said. "The last thing you need is to entertain me or cook dinner for me."

"Don't go," I said. "Please."

He studied me before nodding. "Okay. I can help cook dinner if you want?"

He followed me into the kitchen, a cute grin crossing his

face when I said, "You've told me a few times that you can't cook."

"I can't, but I know how to chop things," he said.

I pointed to the stool at the island. "My preference is to cook without a sous chef, but I'd love it if you kept me company while I cooked."

"Sure." He sat down on the stool. "How was your day?"

"Good. Worked out, finished marking a quiz I gave on Thursday, and then met Tristan for lunch and a movie. Yours?"

"Quiet. I slept in, showered, watched some golf on TV."

"You like golf?" I added some olive oil to the pan and set it on the stove to heat.

"Yeah. Me and my old man play about three times a week. How about you?"

"Never learned." I took the chicken thighs and the vegetables out of the fridge and set them on the counter.

"So, what did Tristan mean with his 'we had a lot to talk about' statement?" Ian said.

I froze with the knife held over the red pepper, thanking God that my back was turned, and Ian couldn't see my face.

Tristan's right. Tell him you can't sleep with him.

I ignored my inner voice and lied to Ian. "He thinks I should get to know someone more before I sleep with them."

"That's a fair point," Ian said.

I chopped the vegetables for the dish, my hands only trembling the tiniest bit.

"Go ahead, ask me anything," Ian said.

"Any siblings?" I put the thighs in the pan.

"Younger sister. You?"

"No, just me."

"Your parents seem great. I know I only met them briefly, but your dad's prank was pretty epic."

I glanced at him over my shoulder. "What did he do?"

"I thought they were you standing behind me, so I said some stuff that made it pretty clear we were more than friends." Ian's face was flushed again. "He pretended they didn't know you were gay."

"Oh my God," I said with a shake of my head as I seasoned the chicken and added it to the pan. "That is so my dad."

"Yeah, it was pretty fucking awful for about thirty seconds before your mom spilled the truth."

I laughed. "Sorry, man. My dad thinks he's funny."

"It was funny," Ian said with his own laugh. "You seem to have a good relationship with your parents."

"I do." Ian hadn't asked but I said, "I came out to them when I was twelve and they've been nothing but supportive about it."

"That's great," Ian said.

The chicken thighs were seared, and I put them on a plate before sauteing the onion and the garlic and then adding the vegetables to the pan. "You worried about your parents finding out you're…"

"Bi?" Ian said.

"So, you've decided to label it?"

He just shrugged. "I don't think it's a bad thing to define what I want or who I am."

"It isn't," I said. "Are you worried about what your parents will say?"

"Nah. They'll be cool about it. Also, they never liked Lori, so anyone I bring home after her, they'll love. My mom actually cried tears of happiness when I told her Lori and I were through."

"Did you always want to be a teacher?"

"I wanted to be a professional athlete or a singer," Ian said.

I grinned at him. "A country singer?"

"Look, I love country music and I'm not gonna hide it anymore," he said with a cute smile.

"So, do you secretly wear a cowboy hat and go to country and western bars to square dance?"

Ian burst into laughter. "Square dance? I think the word you're looking for is line dance, and yes, I've been known to go line dancing from time to time with Rachel. You should try it sometime, you might love it."

"You didn't answer the cowboy hat question," I said.

"You're picturing me in nothing but a cowboy hat right now, aren't you?" Ian said.

"Maybe."

He laughed and a comfortable silence fell over us as I finished prepping dinner. When everything was in the skillet, I joined Ian at the island. "It should take about an hour or so to cook. If you're starving, I've got some apples or raw veggies in the fridge."

"I'm good," Ian said. "So, what else do you want to know about me?"

"It's your turn to ask me a question," I said.

"Describe your idea of a perfect date."

"Hmm, that's a tough one," I said. "I'd have to say April twenty-fifth. Because it's not too hot, not too cold, all you need is a light jacket."

Ian roared with laughter and held out his fist for me to bump. His laughter sent waves of warmth over my body and I didn't stop to think about why I should or shouldn't kiss him. I leaned in, cupped his face, and kissed him.

He returned my kiss, his lips warm and firm and tasting slightly minty, like maybe he'd brushed his teeth right before coming over. The kiss was hot, don't get me wrong, but there was a sweetness to it as well. A sweetness that was pure Ian and just made my attraction to him grow stronger.

You mean your love.

We broke apart and Ian smiled at me. "So, big *Miss Congeniality* fan, huh?"

"Yeah. You too?"

"My little sister made me watch it so many times when we were growing up. I used to act like I hated having to watch it repeatedly but, truthfully, it was one of my favourite movies. Still is."

We were still only inches apart, and Ian pressed another quick kiss against my mouth. "I really enjoyed last night."

"Me too," I said.

"Maybe we could try it again tonight," he said. "Or maybe even get to the main event."

"Maybe," I said, as the warmth in my belly was replaced with dismay.

I sat up straight, incredibly thankful that my cell phone had started buzzing. I pulled it from my pocket. "It's my dad. I'll just be a minute."

Feeling like I'd just dodged a very large fucking bullet, I walked out of the kitchen.

CHAPTER 13

IAN

I finished loading the dishwasher and snuck a look at Will as he put the lid on the leftovers. He looked tired and distracted and even though it was barely seven, I decided it was time for me to leave.

He'd said he had a headache, but was that all it was? Maybe he really hated that I'd come by without calling him first. It was stupid of me to assume that just because I was comfortable with him stopping in unexpectedly at my place, that he would feel the same.

"Hey, Will?"

He paused in snapping on the lid. "Yeah?"

"Dinner was great. Thank you."

"You're welcome."

He put the leftovers in the fridge, and I cleared my throat awkwardly. "Listen, I shouldn't have come by without texting you first. I won't do it again."

He scowled at me. "I told you it was fine, Ian."

Okay, so strike that off the list of what was bothering him.

I decided it did neither of us any good to play twenty questions. "Will you tell me what's wrong?"

He sighed. "I told you, I have a headache and I'm tired."

I pushed away from the counter, not liking the way he tensed when I slid my arms around his waist and pulled him into my embrace. I kneaded the back of his neck. "Do you want me to leave?"

"No," he said. He studied my chin as if he'd never seen it before. "I don't want you to leave, but…"

But he didn't want to have sex with me. It suddenly clicked with crystal clear clarity. I told myself not to read into that. Will had a headache and it wasn't like we hadn't spent plenty of time in bed together this weekend already. Besides, people had different sex drive levels, right? If Will's was lower than mine, that didn't mean he wasn't into me anymore.

I pressed a kiss against his forehead, still kneading the back of his neck gently. "Why don't we just relax tonight and watch some TV? Maybe see if we can get me as addicted to *Justified* as you are? I can't stay super late, I have an early morning volleyball practice with the grade eleven girls, but I could watch a few episodes before I head home."

The tension blew from Will's face with the speed of a category five hurricane. He practically sagged in my embrace as he stared at me. "You sure? You're okay with just… relaxing?"

"I am," I said. "C'mon, let's go watch some hot Timothy Olyphant in a cowboy hat."

"WHAT DO YOU MEAN YOU HAVEN'T HAD SEX WITH WILL yet?" Rachel peered at me from the screen of my phone. She was sitting on her couch and her face was covered in some kind of green mask. "You guys didn't do it last weekend?"

I shook my head and speared some more cold Beefaroni straight from the can and popped it into my mouth.

"Fuck, that's disgusting," Rachel said. "Stop eating that garbage, Ian. Seriously. It's so bad for you."

"Yeah, I know." I tossed the now empty can into the sink. "We didn't have sex last weekend. I mean, we did stuff but no actual fucking. I thought it might happen Sunday night, but Will had a headache and was tired. We just hung out and watched television."

Rachel frowned, the green paste on her face wrinkling into lines on her forehead. "You didn't hook up at all this week?"

"No. He was busy every night this week after work."

"Ian," Rachel's face turned serious, "maybe he's ghosting you in a 'I can't ghost you at work, but I'll ghost you out of my social life,' kind of way."

"He isn't," I said. "We ate lunch together every day in the staff room and he's acting normal. He just hasn't had time to hang out after work."

"That seems weird to me," Rachel said.

"Why? We're not dating. This is just about the sex."

"Then why did you hang out last Sunday without having sex?"

"I don't know, it was a one-off weird thing. Look, it's no big deal, okay? I'm getting together with him later today, and I'm confident that I'll be spending a very enjoyable Saturday afternoon having sex with Will."

"And then it's done," Rachel said.

"Yes."

"Completely. You go back to being just work colleagues."

"Well, probably friends too."

"And you're okay with that?" Rachel leaned in closer to her screen.

"I agreed to it, didn't I?" I realized I was clenching my teeth and my tongue was stuck to the roof of my mouth. I made myself relax with a concentrated effort.

"Doesn't mean you're okay with it now," she said.

"I am," I said. "Even if I wanted more, Will doesn't, and I think he's made that perfectly clear this last week."

"True," Rachel said. "If he was interested in more than just sex, he would have tried to at least spend an evening or two with you this week."

Rachel was right, I knew she was right, so why did I still feel like she'd punched me in the nuts?

"Why do you look like I've punched you in the nuts?" Rachel said.

"I don't," I said. "I'd better go. I'm supposed to be at Will's in an hour and I still need to shower and shave. See you, Rach."

"Bye, honey. Hey, if you want more from Will, you know that's okay to feel that way, right?"

"I don't feel anything for him except lust. And it wouldn't matter how I feel anyway," I said, "not when I know that Will doesn't want more. Besides, even if he did actually want to date or something, I can't do that to him. After what Lori did to me, I'm not in the right headspace to date someone, and that's not fair to Will."

"True," Rachel said. "Look at you being all emotionally and mentally healthy and shit. Good on you, babe."

I laughed. "Yeah, thanks. I really have to go."

"Okay. Love you, bud. Call me tomorrow and tell me how the sex was."

"Love you too, Rach." I ended the video call and set my phone on the counter before staring out the window.

I'd said all the right things to Rachel about not being ready to date Will. About not feeling anything for him other than lust. Now, I just had to convince myself and maybe this sick feeling about never being in Will's bed again after tonight would disappear.

SOMETHING WAS WRONG WITH WILL. EVEN IF I WASN'T weirdly tuned in to his moods already, it was easy to see. He'd invited me over for lunch but barely eaten a thing. He'd hardly said five sentences in the last hour, and he tensed whenever I touched him.

I loaded the last of the dishes in the dishwasher and then reached to dry the pan that Will had finished scrubbing.

"I can do that," he said.

"I don't mind." I dried it and Will put it away in the cupboard.

We stood awkwardly for a few seconds, I never truly understood how *loud* silence could be, until Will cleared his throat. I stared encouragingly at him, but he didn't say anything.

"Do you want to -"

"Let's watch some TV," Will said.

I caught his hand before he could leave the kitchen, hating the way his big body stiffened. "Will, look at me."

He studied me silently and I linked our fingers together. "Tell me what's wrong."

He stared at our entwined hands. "I can't have sex with you, Ian."

The food I'd just eaten turned to a heavy stone in my belly. Dismay washed over me, but under that there was a lack of surprise wasn't there? Despite what I'd told Rachel, a part of me had known this conversation was on its way. I just didn't want to admit it to myself.

"Can't or won't?" I was proud of how steady my voice sounded.

"Does it matter?" Will said.

"Yes. Can't implies there might be something I can do to fix it. Won't says that you don't want me anymore."

He laughed bitterly. "I still want you, Ian. Trust me."

I stepped closer, sliding my arm around his waist and smiling at him. "I want you too. So, tell me why you think you can't do this and maybe I can help find a solution."

"I want more," Will said. "I can't have sex with you knowing that I have to walk away afterward."

"Okay," I said as relief flooded over me. "That's cool. I would be interested in a friends with benefits thing too."

"No," Will pushed away from me, "that isn't what I mean."

He folded his arms across his torso and inhaled deeply. "I want a relationship with you, Ian. I'm not looking for just sex."

"But you said – I mean, you made it perfectly clear that wasn't what you wanted from me," I said.

"I've changed my mind."

"Why?"

"Why do you think? I like you. I like you a lot." Now he was the one to step closer and put his arms around me. He pressed a kiss against my mouth. "We're good together, Ian. We really are. And I think – I hope – you want more too."

Confusion and fear and a little bit of anger jockeyed for control. "You knew I didn't want a relationship, Will. I just got out of a two-year relationship that, frankly, fucked me up. We agreed that this would be just sex between us."

"We did," Will said. "But things change. Don't tell me you don't feel something for me that's more than just lust."

"That isn't the point." I pulled away from him and paced back and forth in the small kitchen.

"That's exactly the point," Will said.

I scowled at him. "No, the point is that I am emotionally fucked up and need time to figure out who I am and what I want from a relationship. I am never being put in a situation again where I'm cheated on."

Will's face reddened. "I am not Lori. Stop comparing me to her. She might have cheated on you but that doesn't mean I will."

"I didn't say that," I protested.

"That's exactly what you just said."

My frustration with Will grew even stronger. "This is really unfair of you. You know that right? We had an agreement and now you're backing out of it just because you…"

"Because I care about you and want more," Will said. "That's the first time that anyone's ever told me it was a bad thing to care about them."

I raked my hand through my hair. "That isn't what I'm saying! What I'm saying is that I'm not ready for a relationship because -"

"Because Lori cheated on you and you think I'll do the same thing," Will said.

"No, that isn't it. Stop putting words in my mouth, Will."

"Then what is it?" Will said. "Because I know you feel more for me than you want to admit and if it's because you're scared, we can take this slow. At least give us a chance to see -"

"I'm not worth it!" I shouted.

Silence descended in the kitchen. Will reached for me and I backed away, shaking my head. "I'm not worth it, Will. Lori cheated on me because I was a terrible boyfriend, all right? She wanted space, I wanted to cling. She wanted to party, I wanted to stay home. She wanted normal sex, I wanted her to fuck me in the ass. She always said that I couldn't compromise, that being in a relationship with me meant always giving in and never getting what she needed. I am fucking lousy at relationships and I deserved to have Lori cheat on me."

"Ian, you aren't a lousy boyfriend."

"You don't know that! You can't possibly know that," I said. "And I can't... I mean, it would kill me if you cheated on me, Will. Even if it was my fault."

"It wasn't your fault," Will said. "Ian, no one is perfect but that doesn't give a person the right to -"

"You don't understand," I said. "I'm done talking about my failures and my humiliations. I can't be with you, Will. Even if," I swallowed hard, "even if that's what I want most."

Will's gaze softened and he reached for me. "Baby, if that's what you want then -"

"I have to go." I pushed past him and headed down the hallway. "I'm sorry, Will. I'm sorry for hurting you, for... I'm sorry."

I shut the door behind me and hurried to my car, climbing behind the wheel and backing out of the driveway as Will stood on the porch. My hands shaking and my throat burning, I drove away without looking back.

CHAPTER 14

IAN

"Patty. It was Patty?" I stared at Joe across his desk. Outside his office window I could see my grade ten boys running laps around the football field. The biology teacher, Randall Cornish, was keeping a close eye on them as they ran.

I'd been puzzled but not worried when Randall joined me in the field and said Joe needed to speak to me. Normally, that would have made me a little anxious, but ever since I'd walked away from Will on Saturday afternoon, I couldn't seem to feel any emotion beyond regret and sorrow.

It'd been less than forty-eight hours since I'd seen him, but fuck, I missed him. I'd spent most of Sunday deliberating on whether or not to send him an apology text, but what good would that do? I still couldn't date him, and that's what he wanted.

I rubbed at my forehead. Honestly, I was as surprised as Will at my outburst, at my insistence that I wasn't good enough, but it was true, wasn't it? I was a lousy boyfriend and my fear that I would be a lousy one to Will and drive him into the arms of another ate at my stomach like battery acid. It was one fuck of an epiphany to have about yourself, and I was still grappling with the enormity of finally truly understanding that Lori wasn't to blame, but me.

Although to be honest, I wished more than anything that it had stayed tucked firmly into my subconscious rather than fighting its way to the light.

"Ian?" Joe had leaned forward, his belly pressing against the edge of his desk. "Are you all right?"

"I don't know," I said. "How do you know it was Patty who spread the rumours and wrote whore on Lori's car?"

Looking deeply uncomfortable, Joe said, "There was an incident over the weekend with Patty and Lori that involved the police."

"What? Is Lori okay?"

"She's fine. They both are. I don't know all the details, but Lori and Frank came home Saturday night to discover that Patty had broken into Frank's house. She had spray painted some very ugly messages all over the walls, and, uh, defecated in their bed."

"How did they know it was her?" I asked.

"She was passed out in the guest room," Joe said.

"Holy shit," I said. "Why did Patty do all this?"

"You know what they say about a woman scorned," Joe said.

"What? Frank and Patty were… Frank cheated on Patty with Lori?" I said.

"Not exactly," Joe said delicately. "I guess, uh, Lori cheated on Patty with Frank."

For the first time since I'd left Will's house on Saturday, a different emotion broke through the fog of despair and regret.

"Are you fucking kidding me? I mean... sorry for the language."

Joe shook his head. "It's quite understandable, Ian. I'm not joking though. I guess Lori and Patty had been sleeping together for the last year or so."

"The last year," I repeated. "So, Lori was cheating on me with Patty and then cheating on Patty with Frank."

Joe nodded. "I guess Patty was still at the school the night you and Frank... argued."

"She was," I said. "She had come on to me in the staff room not ten minutes earlier."

Joe's eyes bulged in surprise, but to his credit, he kept his composure. "I see. Well, apparently, Patty believed that Lori had broken up with you to pursue a full-time relationship with her. Evidently, she overheard you, Lori, and Frank that night. When she realized Lori was also sleeping with Frank, Patty..."

"Lost her mind," I said.

"That's an accurate description," Joe said. "Anyway, as you can imagine, Patty is no longer an employee at the school. Lori's taking a few days off, and I suggest that you take a day or two as well."

"What? Why?" I said.

"Because you look like shit," Joe said bluntly. "It's been a rough few weeks for you, Ian, and I know I'm partially to blame for that. I'd like to formally apologize again for my accusations."

"I get it," I said. "It's fine, Joe."

"It isn't," he said, "but I can only strive to do better in the future. In the meantime, I've arranged to have your classes today and tomorrow covered. Go home, Ian. Get some rest."

"I don't need -"

"You do," Joe said. "I could pack all of my clothes in that

set of luggage you're carrying under your eyes. Go home. We'll see you back here on Wednesday."

I nodded, too stunned and overwhelmed by what I'd just learned to keep arguing. "Okay. Thanks, Joe."

———————

LORI WAS WAITING FOR ME IN THE PARKING LOT WHEN I drove in. I parked in my spot and climbed out of my car, staring cautiously at her as she crossed the lot to join me.

"Hey, Ian." She smiled tentatively at me.

"What are you doing here?" I said. "How did you even know I wasn't at the school?"

"Julie texted me."

"Julie, the social studies teacher?" I said. "I didn't realize you were friends."

Lori just shrugged. "She said that you spoke with Joe and then left the school, and that Randall told her you were taking a couple of days off."

"I am." We were at the front door to the condo building now. "I'll see you around, Lori."

"Ian, wait. Can I come in? Just to talk," Lori said.

"There's nothing left to say between us," I said.

"Please," she pleaded. "Just give me five minutes."

"Fine," I said.

We rode the elevator and walked to my condo in silence. I grabbed two bottles of water from the fridge and set one in front of Lori as she slid onto the stool. She glanced around the condo before taking a sip. "I miss this place."

I sighed. "If you're here to talk about how much you miss the condo that you never stopped complaining about, I think we're done."

"No, that's not it." Lori toyed with the bottle cap from her water before laughing bitterly. "I supposed you know what happened with Patty this weekend."

"Joe told me," I said.

"And if he hadn't, someone else would have," she sighed. "That school is full of gossipy bitches."

I wanted to say that up until today, she'd been one of those gossipy bitches, but kept my mouth shut.

"I'm sorry, Ian," Lori finally said after a few more minutes of silence.

"Sorry for what?" I said. "Sorry for cheating on me with not just one person, but with two? Or sorry for making me feel perverted and sick for wanting something outside the," I made quotation marks with my fingers, "standard idea of sex?"

She flushed and took a big swallow of water. "I didn't sign up to date someone who was gay, Ian."

"Are you fucking kidding me?" I said. "You were fucking Patty for over a year!"

"That's different," Lori said.

"How? How is that different?"

"It just… it just is, okay? Two women together isn't, I mean, it's not gross like two men. Besides, it was just an experiment for me."

"Oh, you are a fucking piece of work, Lori," I scoffed.

"Look, I'm not here to talk about… that, all right?" she said.

"What are you here to talk about then?" I said.

Before she could reply, I sat down on the stool across from her and said, "Why did you cheat on Patty with Frank?"

Lori stared at the counter. "I don't want to talk about it."

"Then leave," I said. "Because I'm not talking shit with you until you answer that goddamn question."

She huffed and gave me her famous Lori pout. I just

shook my head and pointed toward the door. "Goodbye, Lori."

"Fine." She tapped the bottle cap against the island in a quick, hard rhythm. "Patty always had to have her own way. She wouldn't compromise ever, and my needs were never met. I always had to be the one to bend. Frank was a distraction from the pressure that both of you put me under to be a person I wasn't."

I stared at her in a combination of disbelief and 'did she really just say what I think she said'.

"What?" Lori said. "Ian, you asked the reason why."

"You know what's really pathetic, Lori? I actually let you fool me into thinking this was my fault. Let you fool me into believing that I was the one who couldn't compromise."

"You can't," Lori said. "Ian, I love you, but you are an incredibly difficult person to date. You were constantly asking me to do things you wanted to do and didn't even care that it was hard on me."

"Like what?" I said. "Name one thing I asked you to do without caring what you wanted?"

"You made me go to that stupid ceremony and party last May," she said.

"It was my little sister's college graduation," I said. "It was important to her for us to be there."

"I had a headache," she said, "and you didn't even care."

"Oh my God," I said. "I gave you Advil and rubbed your fucking neck and shoulders for an hour before we went to the ceremony. And then I left Kira's party after only half an hour because you wouldn't stop bitching about how you didn't want to be there."

"I had a headache," Lori repeated.

I shook my head. "You're something else, Lori. You really

are. I felt so guilty for most of our relationship, do you know that? All the times you whined at me about how I wouldn't compromise because I didn't want to go to the fucking bar for the seventh weekend in a row. Or how I was crowding you and not giving you personal space because I wanted to have dinner with you after you'd spent the entire weekend with your girlfriends."

Her face drew down in a pout. "Stop making me feel guilty for needing my alone time, Ian."

"I'm not." I laughed. "My God, I can't believe how fucking stupid I am. All this time, I've let myself believe that you were right, when it's you who can't compromise. I actually thought that I deserved to be cheated on by you. But it isn't me, it's you. You're the bad person, Lori. You cheated on me, on Patty, and on Frank. Because there's something wrong with you. I just couldn't see that until now. Talk about being blinded by pussy."

"Don't be crude, Ian!" Lori snapped. "That's not who you are."

"You have no idea who I am," I said.

She took a deep breath. "You're right, but I still love you, and I want you back. Give me a chance to get to know the real you."

And here I'd thought finding out Lori was fucking Patty would be my biggest shock of the day.

"You're with Frank," I said.

She stared down at her lap. "Not anymore. We broke up last night."

"Because Patty shit in his bed?" I said.

She stared furiously at me. "Stop being an asshole." She rubbed at her temples. "Look, I'm sorry, okay? Truly I am. Give me a second chance."

"No fucking way."

Surprise flickered across her face. "But... but you have to, Ian."

"I don't have to do anything."

"You love me," she said.

"No, I don't."

Her lower lip started to tremble, and I shrugged. "Go ahead and cry. It won't change my mind."

"I don't have a place to stay," she said. "You really would let me sleep in my car?"

I rolled my eyes. "You don't have to sleep in your car. There's another option. It's called a motel, Lori."

"Ian... you have to take me back," she said. "You just have to."

"No, I don't. Leave."

"Ian -"

"Leave," I repeated. "I am never getting back together with you. Ever, Lori. Get that through your skull."

She slammed her half-empty water bottle down on the island in a fit of temper. "Fine! I'm too good for you anyway."

"You're too something," I said.

She stalked to the door. "You'll never find anyone better than me."

"I already have," I said.

She slammed the door shut and I slumped against the island, my blood whooshing in my ears. Jesus, I felt like I'd just been through twelve rounds of a championship boxing match. I took a few deep breaths. Despite my newfound revelation, the weight was still on my chest, the sick feeling still rolling in my stomach. It wouldn't leave.

Not until I talked to Will.

CHAPTER 15

WILL

I was home barely fifteen minutes before I grabbed my car keys. I couldn't sit here in my goddamn house. Not after what I'd heard today. Ian didn't want a relationship with me, I knew that, but I'd be damned if I let him sit alone after finding out his girlfriend had cheated on him with two people. If he told me to leave, I would leave, but I wanted to give him the chance to let me be a friend to him tonight. He obviously needed it. I'd never seen Ian take so much as a sick day, let alone two personal days.

I didn't bother with my jacket. Just grabbed my phone and headed for the front door. I should probably text Ian first, but texting him would give him the opportunity to tell me to stay home. If I was already at his place, maybe he'd be more willing to let me sit with him for a bit.

I yanked open the door and staggered back, a startled scream escaping my throat. "What the fuck?"

"Uh, hi." Ian lowered his arm. "Man, this happens a lot to us, huh?"

"Ian, what – what are you doing here?"

He cleared his throat. "I wanted to talk to you, but if you're headed out, I can come back later. Or maybe we could have coffee tomorrow after work?"

"I was on my way to your house," I said stupidly.

"You were?"

I nodded and his small smile made the clamp that seemed to be permanently squeezing my heart, loosen a little.

"That's cool. Can I come in?"

"Yes, of course." I moved back, watching as Ian stepped inside and closed the door behind him.

I'd never expected to see him in my house again and I could hear the giddiness in my voice when I said, "Come into the kitchen. You want a beer?"

"Shit, yeah," he said. "It's been a day."

I opened two beers and handed one to him. Ian sat at the island and, after a moment's hesitation, I sat on the stool next to his.

He held up his beer bottle. "To cheating ex-girlfriends."

It was an odd thing to toast, but I clinked my bottle against his and we both drank.

Ian studied me and I couldn't help myself. "That was a weird toast."

He laughed. "Maybe, but it's because of Lori that I'm here. I suppose you heard what happened?"

I nodded. "The teachers aren't exactly being discreet about it."

"Students know yet?"

"I don't think so. I'm sorry, Ian."

"For what?"

"Well, that Lori cheated on you with Frank and Patty. Sorry that she made you feel abnormal and wrong for wanting something that she herself was doing."

"You know what? I'm glad she was cheating with two people."

"Why?" I said.

"Because it helped me realize that she was wrong about me. That, yeah, maybe I'm not perfect, but I'm not the person she kept telling me I was."

"You're not," I said.

"I know that now. I feel stupid for allowing myself to believe her lies."

"Don't. You loved her, and sometimes love makes people do dumb things," I said.

Ian smiled a little and when he reached for my hand, I linked our fingers together and held tight. He studied me for a moment before saying, "Why were you coming to my house?"

"I was worried about you," I said. "I didn't want you to be alone."

"Even after the horrible things I said to you?" Ian said.

"You were upset. I'd hurt you and I'm sor-"

He shook his head. "No, don't say you're sorry. I need to be the one to say sorry. I'm sorry for pushing you away, Will. Sorry for refusing to admit that you were right, and I wanted more with you too. I was afraid and confused, but that's no excuse."

He rubbed his thumb along my knuckle. "I'm here to ask if you'll give me another chance. I want to date you, Will. I want to get to know you and show you who I am. And I know that maybe you won't like me once you find out who the real me is, but I'm willing to take that risk. Because I promise you, I will work really hard to be a good, no, a *great*, boyfriend."

I could feel the huge smile breaking out on my face. "You don't need to work nearly as hard as you think you do, Ian."

He squeezed my hand. "So, does this mean you'll give me another shot?"

"Oh, fuck yes," I said.

"Good." He hesitated and then started to lean forward. I met him halfway and when his lips touched mine, that clamp around my heart finally fell off. I hooked my arm around his neck and pulled him in closer, our chests touching, and our arms locked around each other as we kissed hungrily.

"Fuck, I've missed you," Ian said when we came up for air.

"I've missed you too." I rested my forehead against his. "Are you hungry? I could make us dinner."

"You could," Ian said. "Or we could go up to your bedroom and fuck, and then order pizza afterward."

I couldn't help but laugh. "That is a viable option."

"So, what will it be? Option A or B?"

"B," I said. "Definitely option B."

"I was hoping you'd say that." Still holding my hand, Ian slid off the stool. I followed him as eagerly as a puppy to my bedroom.

We stripped quickly, both of us too impatient to undress each other.

When we were naked, I pulled Ian into my arms and kissed him again. Despite how much I wanted to be in his beautiful ass, I made myself slow down, savour every brush of his tongue against mine, the unique taste that was Ian and only Ian.

He moaned into my mouth, his hips arching when I reached between us and stroked his hard dick. "Fuck, Will, that feels so good. I want you."

"I want you too," I said. Before he could stop me, I was sitting on the bed and pulling his hips toward me. I grasped the base of his dick and sucked on the head, cleaning away the precum leaking from the slit.

Ian cried my name, his hands clutching in my hair and his hips jerking in surprise. "Oh fuck, oh fuck, that feels so good."

I sucked more of him into my throat, going deep until the head of his cock pressed against the back of my throat before retreating. Ignoring Ian's soft cries to slow down or he would cum, I set a brisk pace of sucking, bobbing my head back and forth over Ian's magnificent cock, using my tongue to tease out every curse word in the book from Ian's mouth.

He thrust back and forth, his head thrown back and the long naked length of his body in full display for my hungry gaze.

"I'm so close, Will," Ian moaned. "Honey, I'm so close."

I released him long enough to spit on my fingers before taking his cock into my mouth again. He gasped and groaned, his hips rocking back and forth as I sucked hard. I slid my hand around to his ass and pressed my saliva coated finger against his tight hole.

He cried out and I made a grunt of satisfaction when my finger slipped past the ring of muscles. Ian's hands tightened in my hair and it took only one brush of my finger across his prostate to make him lose complete control.

He shouted my name, his hands clutching my skull, his cock swelling in my mouth and then releasing its load down my throat. I swallowed and swallowed again, relishing in the taste of him as he shivered and jerked and moaned.

When he was empty, I released his cock and slid my finger out of his ass. Ian was swaying on his feet and I quickly stood and helped him to lie on the bed.

When he was sprawled on his back in the middle of the bed, I grabbed the lube from the nightstand. My breath hissing out between my teeth at the sensation, I coated my aching dick with lube before kneeling between Ian's muscled thighs.

"Baby, look at me," I said.

Ian cracked open one eye. "Fuck, that was so good, Will."

I rubbed his thigh before pouring lube into my hand. "Spread your legs for me, baby."

He spread his legs, making a little gasp when I coated his hole with the cool lube. I warmed it up with my fingers and then poured more lube around his hole before sliding two fingers inside of him. I stretched him gently for a few minutes, watching his face as I did so.

My cock was aching and I could barely think straight, but I wanted it to be good for Ian, so I took my time, adding more lube and adding a third finger.

Ian opened his eyes and smiled at me. "I'm ready, honey."

<hr>

IAN

DESPITE JUST HAVING THE BEST DAMN ORGASM OF MY LIFE, I was still horny as hell for Will's cock. And while I appreciated everything he was doing to prepare me, if he didn't fuck me soon, I was going to lose my mind.

I smiled up at Will. "I'm ready, honey."

"You sure?" he said. "We can wait if you're not."

"No more waiting," I said. "Unless you're trying to torment me?"

He grinned, the look in those dark eyes of his sending shivers of need up and down my spine. "I like the idea of tormenting you, but maybe after I've fucked this gorgeous ass a few times."

His hands slipped around my thighs and pushed. I brought my legs back, appreciating the assist from Will when he pressed on the backs of my thighs with his warm hands.

He lined his cock up at my hole, stopping with the head resting against it. "You're sure?"

"Oh my God," I said. "Stop talking and fuck me, Will."

He laughed and I blew out my breath and pushed back against Will when he pressed his cock against my hole. There was pressure and a little pain, but I took another few deep breaths as Will rubbed my thighs. "You're doing great, baby. Push against me again."

I did what he asked and grunted when the head of Will's cock breached my tight ring of muscle. Will stopped immediately, rubbing my thighs and watching my face. "Okay?"

"Yeah," I said. "Yeah, it's good. Give me more."

He groaned quietly and pushed forward. I bit my bottom lip at the delicious stretch and burn as Will's cock moved slowly into me. To my surprise, it only took a few more pushes before Will's considerable dick was buried to the balls in my ass.

"Oh God," I said.

"Too much?" Will's face was tense, and I could see the need etched into it.

I shook my head. "No, it's… it's really good. Fuck, I'm getting hard again."

We both looked down at my cock. I'd never had a recovery time of less than ten minutes before and Will made a low sound of need as he studied my half-hard cock. "Touch yourself, baby."

I reached down and stroked myself slowly, concentrating on how good it felt as Will made a few slow thrusts in my ass.

"You can go harder," I gasped as I stroked my now fully erect cock.

"Thank fuck," Will mumbled.

My laugh turned into a moan of desire when Will thrust hard. Still rubbing my dick, I rocked my hips, meeting each of his thrusts as the look on his face turned to one of desperate need.

"Fuck," he said. "You're so fucking tight. I am not going to last."

I slid my thumb across the head of my cock, a hard beat of pleasure made my balls tighten. The sound of our coupling, the slap of Will's heavy balls against my ass, the look on his face as he drove harder and deeper had me on the edge of a second orgasm, just like that.

I jacked myself hard as Will shifted me slightly and changed the angle of his thrusts.

"Oh fuck!" I shouted when his cock rubbed across that lightning bolt of a spot in my ass. "Oh fuck, I'm gonna cum!"

I'd barely gotten the words out before I shot my load, the pleasure of Will's fucking and the touch of my own hand too much for me. Will shouted my name and drove in and out of me with hard and erratic thrusts before his body stiffened and his head fell back.

His hands tightened around my thighs and his body shook as he came deep inside my ass. I gasped in some air, the pleasure finally beginning to ebb enough for me to breathe again. I closed my eyes as Will pulled out and then collapsed on his side next to me.

I could hear his harsh breathing as I stared at the lights exploding in the darkness behind my closed lids.

"Ian," Will gasped, "you okay?"

"Yeah," I gasped in return. "You?"

"I may never be the same again."

I cracked open one eye and grinned at him. "I think that went well. How about you?"

He slung one thigh over mine and an arm around my waist. "Baby, that was the best fucking fuck of my life."

I laughed. "Wow, I had no idea you were such a romantic."

He chuckled before kissing the side of my neck. "You're amazing."

"So, are you," I said.

He smiled and closed his eyes, curling into me and holding me tight. We cuddled in silence for a few minutes before Will, his voice low and filled with a soft warmth, said, "I love you, Ian."

"I love you too."

He opened his eyes and half sat up, staring earnestly at me. "You don't have to say it back if you don't -"

"I mean it," I said. "I wouldn't say it if I didn't."

He pressed a kiss against my mouth. "I know it's probably too soon to be saying it, but I needed you to know."

"I'm glad you did," I said. "Because I love you Will Matthews, and I don't plan on ever letting you go."

He ran his thumb over my bottom lip. "Good, because you're mine, Ian Smith."

"I'm yours," I said. "Now, what do you say we order some pizza, watch an episode or two of Timothy Olyphant in tight jeans, and then come back here and fuck each other's brains out?"

Will's smile widened. "Perfect. Absolutely perfect."

Please enjoy an excerpt from Book Two in the Temptation Series, "Tease".

Tristan

"Shepherd's gonna kill him."

"He's not gonna kill him. He's gonna *fire* him, but he won't kill him."

I stared at the copy of the invoice in my hand, my stomach queasy and my mind already halfway to packing up my shit. Behind me, Roger and Jeff continued to squabble about whether Shepherd would kill me or fire me.

My money was on both. First, Shepherd would fire me, then he'd kill me.

"I'm really sorry, Tristan." MaryBeth looked as nauseous as I felt.

"It's not your fault," I said. "I drew up the invoice."

"Yeah, but I thought it seemed too low when I was ringing it through for the customer. I should have double-checked with you." The pretty brunette looked close to tears.

I shook my head. "It's not your job to double-check my work."

"I'd better get back," MaryBeth said. "I can't hear the phone out here."

She left the bay, walking past the two cars currently on the lifts and the long counter of tools to get to the side door that led into the reception area.

"Maybe," Jeff said, "Shepherd will just beat the shit out of Tristan. I mean, he did used to be a boxer back in the day, right? They solve shit with their fists, yeah?"

"He hasn't boxed in over a decade," Roger said.

"Yeah, but he still works out at the boxing gym over on Mayhill," Jeff said. "Plus, it's not like he's let himself go or anything. The guy's solid muscle."

"Doesn't mean he's gonna beat the shit out of Tristan," Roger said with a disgusted snort. He'd been working at the shop since Shepherd first opened the place and, much like Shepherd, he didn't suffer any fools. "Fuck, Jeff, are you just that stupid or are you high today? Shepherd runs a respectable business. He's not gonna beat up an employee."

Roger turned his gaze to me. "But you are gonna get fired."

I grimaced and my hand crumpled up the edge of the invoice when Shepherd's deep voice said, "Why am I firing you?"

I turned, staring uneasily at Shepherd as Roger and Jeff suddenly found shit to do on the far side of the bay. Shepherd had walked in through the open door of the bay and was holding a brown paper bag with the words 'The Vigilant Vegan" imprinted on the side. His t-shirt was tight across his broad chest, his jeans clung to his thick thighs, and, like usual, he had a two-day growth of dark hair on his jaw. The man always had the perfect damn amount of stubble.

Normally, I would be hard-pressed to look away from that stubble, to stop imagining what it might feel like brushing against certain sensitive spots on my body, but right now? At this moment, my usual urge to lust after my boss like a horny llama had disappeared. And all it took was the certainty that I was about to lose my damn job.

"We can talk after you eat lunch," I said. Partly because I didn't want to ruin Shepherd's lunch, and partly because maybe if I had even half an hour more, I'd come up with a convincing argument for why Shepherd shouldn't fire me.

Not a chance, buddy. You're so losing your job today.

Shepherd studied me before crooking his head at his office. "Talk to me while I'm eating."

He turned and headed toward the small hole in the wall that functioned as his office. It had two doors, one accessed through reception, just past the bathroom and storage closet, and the other door leading straight into the bay.

My stomach churning up bile, I followed Shepherd across the bay, picking my way past the third empty lift, the diagnostic equipment lined up neatly against the wall, and the tools from Roger's toolbox that he'd left scattered on the floor.

"Roger, pick up your fucking tools before I toss them in the dumpster," Shepherd said as I stepped over them.

"You got it, boss," Roger said. Wiping at the grease on his fingers, Roger ambled over to the toolbox, giving me a sympathetic look as he squatted to pick up the wrenches.

My back sweating, I followed Shepherd into the office.

"Close the door." Shepherd sat down behind his desk and cleared a space free of the piles of work orders that always seemed to cover his desk. Shepherd's office was a tornado of car parts, tools, paperwork, and... honestly, he could have had anything hidden under all the papers and tools ... holy shit, was that a Barbie doll?... piled on the floor surrounding his desk. I had an idea that the last time Shepherd cleaned his office or filed anything was a decade ago when the shop first opened.

I shut the door, dimming the whir of the oscillating fans on the wall in the bay, Roger's whistling, and the idling engine of the car Jeff had just pulled into the empty spot in the bay. Still holding the invoice in my hand, I sat in the rusted folding chair in front of Shepherd's desk. Shepherd pulled a sandwich out of the bag. From the looks of it, it was the Vigilant Vegan's rainbow veggie sandwich.

I felt a small pang of regret. Before I'd quit the family business, the Vigilant Vegan was one of my favourite restaurants, their rainbow veggie sandwich one of my go-to's for ordering. Unfortunately, my eating-out budget had dried up significantly in the last few years.

"Tell me why I'm firing you," Shepherd said then bit into his sandwich.

The scent of the restaurant's special – *delicious* – sauce drifted to me. Normally I'd be salivating at this point. My total lack of hunger only hammered down the reality that while I could pretend to be hopeful, I knew I was about to be fired.

Christ. I was only halfway through my apprenticeship, and I was getting fired from my first job. I'd never find another shop to take me on as an apprentice. My new career was over before it even started.

Shepherd stared pointedly at me as he chewed.

I cleared my throat. "I invoiced Trevor Warner incorrectly. Forgot to add on some stuff. He paid and left before I realized my mistake."

Now the sweat was popping up on my forehead. Shepherd took another bite of his sandwich, chewed, and swallowed. "How much did you forget to bill?"

"A significant amount," I said.

Shepherd eyed me over the sandwich. "How significant?"

Afraid I'd barf if I said anything else, I handed over the now wrinkled and slightly damp invoice copy before wiping my sweaty palms on my coveralls. I watched Shepherd's face as he read over the invoice. To my surprise, the anger I expected to wash over Shepherd's face didn't appear.

Afraid Shepherd hadn't realized what I forgot to bill, I said, "I missed the diagnostic fee and -"

"Your labour costs. I can read," Shepherd said.

He set the sandwich down on the paper wrapper and opened the bottle of water sitting on his desk. He took a drink and then leaned back in his chair, staring steadily at me.

"What were you doing when you were invoicing that caused you to make such a stupid mistake?"

I winced, but what was I expecting? It was a stupid mistake. What kind of asshole forgot to bill for their time? This might be my first job as a mechanic, but I'd been working here for over six months now. I had no fucking excuse.

Sure you do. You were daydreaming about what it might be like to have Shepherd bend you over his desk and fuck you. Remember?

Dull heat climbed up my neck. I cleared my throat again as Shepherd continued to stare at me. He was waiting for an answer, but somehow I didn't think admitting that I was thinking about being fucked by Shepherd, would help save my job.

Might as well admit it, your ass is fired either way.

My inner voice was probably right, but, not including my best friend Will, I would take my inappropriate crush on my boss to my fucking grave before I admitted it to anyone.

———

ABOUT THE AUTHOR

Evelyn Bloom writes bold and sexy M/M romances that always end in happily ever after.

When not writing, her free time consists of reading, embroidering naughty art, and watching Netflix. She has a serious addiction to lip balm, nineties boy bands, and learning curse words in multiple languages.

For more information about Evelyn, check out her website at

www.evelynbloom.com

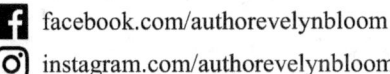

facebook.com/authorevelynbloom
instagram.com/authorevelynbloom

ALSO BY EVELYN BLOOM

Temptation Series

Tempt

Tease

Taste